HIDEAWAY

HIDEAWAY

RACHEL LACEY

VINO &
VERITAS

HeartEyes
Press

PHOEBE

The door closed behind me with a soft click, and I leaned against it, one hand clasped around the handle of my suitcase. The house looked exactly like I remembered, with floral-papered walls and thick piled carpet that squished beneath my shoes. It smelled the same too, spicy undertones of the incense my grandma used to burn, mixed with the musky scent of dogs. I almost expected to hear Grandma's voice calling from the kitchen and Comet's friendly bark as he rushed to greet me.

Today, the house was silent. Dust motes danced in the air where a shaft of sunlight cut across the entryway from the front window. And behind the familiar scents, there was a staleness that came from the house having been closed up for more than six months. I pushed the suitcase ahead of me as I walked into the living room. Its wheels snagged in the thick carpet, and I stumbled against it, banging my shin.

"Dammit," I whispered, rubbing my leg. My voice disturbed the absolute silence inside the house. I wasn't used to quiet, having just left Boston and then singing along to my favorite music in the car during my drive to Vermont. My ears seemed to ring with the absence of noise. This was why I'd come, though, not only to clean out my grandmother's home, but to be alone, to hide out here in the middle of nowhere while I waited for the shit-storm back home to die down.

After three and a half hours in the car, my bladder was pretty unhappy with me, so I went down the hall to the guest bathroom, leaving my suitcase stuck in the carpet. The little bowl of potpourri by the sink was still there, keeping the room fresh despite the layer of dust on the surfaces. I freshened up, avoiding my reflection in the mirror. I knew what I'd see if I looked. My eyes were shadowed from too many sleepless nights, my curly hair limp from having dried in a ponytail during my drive. My clothes were probably wrinkled too.

With a sigh, I walked to the living room to retrieve my suit-case, hit by an unexpected wave of nostalgia as I swept my gaze around the room. My grandma's shelves were filled with the same family photos and knickknacks that had been here for as long as I could remember. There was the sparkly rock I'd brought home from a hike when I was seven, sitting proudly next to a photo of me and my grandma.

"I miss you, Grandma," I whispered. She'd died in her sleep last fall, taken without warning by a massive heart attack. I'd always thought that was the best way to go, except she'd been way too young and none of us had gotten the chance to say good-bye. The door to her bedroom was closed now, and I couldn't bring myself to open it, afraid of what I might find. Were her glasses still sitting beside the bed? Had anyone washed the sheets?

Instead, I pushed my suitcase to the guest room across the hall, the room that had been mine for so many summer vacations during my youth. It looked the same too, with a blue-striped quilt on the bed and white lace curtains, although the air here was unpleasantly stuffy.

I went to the window and unlatched it, giving it a push. Nothing happened. This window had always been tricky. I crouched, lifting from my knees as I pushed upward, finally raising the window a few inches with a dull squeak. Fresh air flowed into the room, warm and lightly scented by my grandmother's rosebushes.

That was a pleasant surprise. I'd been afraid they might have died, left unattended during a harsh Vermont winter. But as I gazed out the window, the backyard looked well-tended. The grass was recently mowed, and the rosebushes I could see from the window were neatly pruned. Had my dad hired someone to keep the place up? If he had, he hadn't mentioned it to me.

I turned away from the window, and my gaze caught on a framed photo on the dresser of two little girls with their arms around each other as they twirled in a field of tall grass. That field was just through the woods out back, and those girls…

I pressed a hand to my heart. I'd come here for an escape, but I'd forgotten how many memories this house held, memories I wasn't ready to face yet. I sat on the bed and checked my phone, finding texts from my best friends Courtney and Emily, as well as one from my mom, all checking to make sure I'd arrived safely.

I miss you already, Courtney had written. *FaceTime later?*

Sending you so many hugs, Emily said.

Drive safely, and let me know when you get there, from my mom.

After sending each of them a quick reply, I left my suitcase in the bedroom and went down the hall to the kitchen for a glass of water. The dishes were all clean and put in their right places. Who had done that? Had my dad cleaned the house when we'd come up for the funeral in November? I'd stayed behind at the hotel when he came here, not ready to see this place without Margery in it.

I filled a glass at the sink and gulped down about half of it, parched from my drive. Then I peeked into the fridge, not sure whether it would be full of old, spoiled food, but it was empty. I'd have to go shopping before dinner. In fact, I was already hungry, but I wasn't ready to get back in the car just yet.

Instead, I put my glass in the sink and went out the kitchen door, descending three worn wooden steps onto the patio. The rosebushes that ran along the back of the house bloomed with big pink, red, and white blossoms. More roses climbed a trellis over the patio, with two white Adirondack chairs beneath it.

A path ran down to the stream at the edge of the yard, where a small wooden bridge connected it to the hiking trail leading into the woods. As a girl, I had loved to explore those woods. Were the trails I'd tromped down so many times still there?

As I inhaled the fresh country air, I felt myself relaxing for the first time in weeks. This was exactly why I'd come to Vermont. I needed the peace and quiet here, the solitude, far from the stress of the city. I needed to be alone for a little while. I'd even deleted all the social media apps from my phone, hoping that by the time I reconnected with the larger world, my notifications would no longer be a hotbed of attention I'd never asked for or wanted.

Something moved in my peripheral vision, and I turned just as an animal rushed out of the woods, dashing toward me. I inhaled, adrenaline bursting through my veins as the shaggy black creature crossed the yard, my mind screaming *bear* a moment before it barked.

Oh, thank God.

The dog ran at me, and I didn't even have a chance to recover from my shock before it planted its front paws on my leg, tail wagging. It was enormous, with bushy black fur like a…well, like a bear.

"Jesus," I muttered as I gave it a cautious pat. I liked dogs, but the way this one came racing out of the woods so unexpectedly had scared me. My heart was still pounding. Was it a stray? There was a red collar around its neck, so maybe not. Before I could look for tags, I heard a woman's voice calling from the direction of the hiking trail.

"Minnie!"

The dog turned its head to stare in the direction of what was probably its owner calling for it, but could an animal this big really be named Minnie? I gave it a gentle nudge since its front paws were still propped against my leg, and it dropped to all fours, panting.

4

I frowned. This was private property. Why was someone hiking on my grandmother's land? That was rude, even if the house had sat vacant for a while.

"Minnie!" the woman called again, and the dog dashed in her direction, letting out an excited bark.

I planted my hands on my hips as a tall woman with hair the color of cinnamon came striding out of the woods with another dog at her side. My heart—which was still pounding—lurched for an entirely different reason, because *oh*, I knew that stride, that smile, that hair.

I'd known her as a little girl, skipping through the field on the other end of this trail, and for one memorable summer when we were sixteen, she'd been more than my best friend. She'd been my first love, the girl whose kiss made me realize I didn't like boys.

I swallowed roughly, my throat gone dry. "Taylor?"

2

TAYLOR

I paused with one hand holding Blue's leash, raising the other to shield my eyes as I stared at the woman standing behind Margery Shaw's house. I'd been waiting for months to run into someone from the Shaw family, hoping to see a For Sale sign in the yard so I would finally get the chance to buy this house. But out of all the scenarios I'd envisioned, I had never expected to see this particular person.

I lifted my chin. "Phoebe?"

Phoebe nodded, reaching up to tuck a brown curl behind her ear. My chest tightened, memories and emotions rising inside me, because she looked so much the same. She was older now, of course. We both were. But in her blue cotton dress, hair piled in a messy ponytail on her head, she looked so much like the Phoebe who'd been my best friend, the Phoebe I'd fallen in love with, the Phoebe who'd broken my heart.

Minnie ran toward her, thrilled to have found a new friend here on Margery's property. The Lab mix was hopelessly enthusiastic. So was I, for that matter. We were a perfect match. Phoebe and me, on the other hand? Not so much.

"I wasn't expecting to see you here," I said, relieved that my voice sounded calm and steady.

"I could say the same thing." Phoebe crossed her arms over her chest. "This is private property, you know?"

Seriously, this was the way she wanted to play it? After all these years, she was going to treat me like an intruder on her grandmother's property?

"You know perfectly well that I know whose land this is," I told her. "I've probably spent more time here than you have. I trimmed Margery's rosebushes when her arthritis acted up. I walked her dog and sat with her in the evenings to drink tea and talk about life. She welcomed me to walk my dogs here any time I wanted, and I didn't think that offer had been rescinded, especially since I've been keeping the place up while I waited for your family to list it for sale."

Phoebe glanced at the meticulously trimmed rosebushes, having the good grace to look sheepish. "I didn't know that was you."

"It's me," I confirmed. "I couldn't bear to see her rosebushes die off. You know how important they were to her. It seemed the least I could do after everything she did for me."

"I'm sorry." Phoebe looked up and met my gaze, maybe for the first time since the summer we were sixteen. "I wasn't expecting to see anyone hiking on my grandmother's property, and especially not you."

"You're the last person I expected to see today too," I said, forcing myself not to look away beneath her intense gaze. She'd always done that, ever since we were little. I'd felt like she was staring straight into my soul, and for a long time, I'd thought she belonged there. Soulmates. As it turned out, I'd been wrong.

"I just got here," Phoebe said. She looked tired, now that I was paying attention. Maybe even sad. Why was she here, after all these years?

"Come to clear the place out?" I asked. It had been six months since Margery passed away, so it was certainly time.

"Something like that," she said, looking down as Minnie

bounded up to her with a stick in her mouth, dropping it at Phoebe's feet.

"Word of caution. If you throw it once, you'll have to throw it a hundred times," I told her, forcing a polite smile onto my face, because if I was going to successfully lobby to buy this place, I needed to make nice with the current owner. Our personal history was irrelevant.

Phoebe bent and chucked the stick across the yard, earning her Minnie's undying devotion. "This dog is really named Minnie?"

"Ironic, right?" I said. "She was the runt of her litter, believe it or not. Their foster mom gave them all Disney-themed names."

"Not surprised you adopted her. You were always trying to take in strays when we were growing up." She gave me a hesitant smile as Minnie dropped the stick at her feet again, tail wagging enthusiastically.

"I actually work at the shelter now."

"Really?" Phoebe's smile looked more genuine now. "That sounds like your dream job. Good for you."

"It is, and thanks."

Blue whined, and I looked down at him. The beagle mix watched me with questioning eyes. I couldn't believe I was standing here talking to Phoebe Shaw either. I steeled myself as I looked back up. I wasn't interested in polite chitchat with this woman, but there was one thing she could do for me.

"Are you here to put the cabin up for sale?" I asked.

"No."

Ugh. That was disappointing, but I still couldn't let this opportunity go to waste. "Well, when the time comes, will you please keep me in mind? I was close with Margery, and I love this property. I'd love to buy it, and I'm willing to pay a fair market price. I could save your family the hassle of having to hire a Realtor and fix it up. I love it just the way it is."

"I would, but we aren't going to put it up for sale," Phoebe said as Minnie dropped the stick at her feet again.

"Why not?" It didn't make sense to keep the cabin if no one

was living in it, unless…oh God. I hoped like hell Phoebe wasn't about to tell me she was moving to Vermont.

"My dad's going to use it as a rental property," she said.

"What? Why?"

"So he can keep it in the family," she told me. "He grew up here, you know? And so did I, at least part-time."

"Oh no," I blurted. "But who will take care of it? The rosebushes? The trails out back?"

"My dad will hire someone, I imagine," Phoebe said, attempting to ignore Minnie as she nudged the stick against her shoe.

"Please reconsider," I said. "Name a price, and I'll do my best to meet it."

"We're not going to sell it," she said, and when she met my gaze this time, I saw something new in her expression. Phoebe wasn't sixteen anymore. She was a twenty-nine-year-old woman who'd been working at some kind of corporate job in Boston for the last seven years. Finance, I thought. "I'm just here for a few weeks to fix it up to rent."

This was just business to her. She hadn't visited her grandmother very often the last few years. Why hadn't she? Had the family even asked Margery what she wanted? Surely, she wouldn't have wanted her home to be a party pad for tourists.

"This is a mistake," I said.

"That's your opinion," Phoebe said. "But in the meantime, this house isn't sitting vacant anymore, so you should probably find a new place to walk your dogs."

I gaped at her for a moment before my temper kicked in. "Wow, not even a thank-you for keeping the place up?"

"Taylor…"

But I didn't want to hear it. I patted my thigh, calling Minnie to me. She picked up her stick and trotted over, tail wagging. I headed around the side of the house, past the purplish-blue Nissan sedan in the driveway that must be Phoebe's. Minnie trotted over to sniff the tires before following me onto the street.

Mountain Laurel Road was barely wide enough for two cars, so I clipped Minnie's leash onto her collar to keep her close for the walk to my parents' house.

Usually, I drove here to hike, but since my parents lived just up the road and I was joining them for dinner tonight, I'd parked there today and walked. The proximity to my parents was another reason I'd hoped to buy Margery's house. I'd worked hard the last few years to save up for a place of my own, and after Margery passed away last fall, I'd realized how perfect her cabin would be for me. It had been my home away from home growing up and had one of my favorite hiking trails right on the property.

Maybe it wasn't Phoebe's fault that her father had decided to use it as a rental property, but this felt a little bit like being rejected by her all over again. My face flushed hot. She certainly hadn't needed to take an attitude with me about it, especially after the way she'd treated me thirteen years ago. If anything, she should have been apologizing.

I tugged the dogs closer as a car went past on the road, stirring the air around us. Blue pinned his ears against his head, pressing his shoulder against my thigh. He was my shy guy, my foster dog. Currently, I could only foster one dog at the time while I was living in an apartment. Once I had a house of my own, I could keep as many fosters as I wanted.

If only I wasn't going to have to restart my house hunt from scratch…

I sighed as I turned into my parents' driveway, releasing Minnie from her leash so she could bound ahead of me up the front steps to the house. I followed with Blue, grabbing the stick from her mouth before I opened the door. She knew better than to try to bring it in the house.

"It's me," I called, giving Blue a reassuring rub. I walked toward the kitchen, where my mom was finishing up dinner. Minnie raced around the corner to greet her while Blue stayed by my side.

"How was your hike?" Mom asked as I entered the kitchen.

"Good." I reached for the bowl my parents kept for my dogs. I filled it with water and set it on the mat on the floor. "I bumped into Phoebe Shaw while I was there, though."

"I hadn't heard she was back in town," my mom said, drying her hands on a dish towel. "Are the Shaws finally putting the cabin on the market?"

I shook my head, watching Minnie as she drank. My mom didn't know Phoebe and I had been high school sweethearts. No one knew, which meant I couldn't even properly vent about all the ways this sucked. "She says they're going to use it as a rental property."

Mom frowned as she slipped oven mitts onto her hands and bent to pull the casserole out of the oven. "Oh, Taylor, I'm sorry. I know how much you were hoping to buy it."

I sighed. "Yeah. I'm pretty disappointed."

"Well, it's time to call Matty, then," she said, naming a long-time family friend who was a Realtor. "He'll find you something just as good."

"You're right," I said, even though I already knew there weren't any other houses for sale within walking distance of my parents. I mean, I didn't *have* to live near them, but we'd always been close, and I liked the idea of being able to drop by whenever I liked, and vice versa. Maybe I should ask Phoebe to reconsider...

"Will you tell your father dinner's ready?"

"Yep." I headed for the back door, knowing without asking that I'd find my dad tinkering in his garden. It was his happy place, especially after a long day at the office. "Hi Dad," I called as I crossed the yard to find him crouched in the garden, examining a row of green spouts. "What's growing this early in the season?"

"Snow peas," he told me as he stood, bracing his hands against his thighs. He wore faded jeans and a Moo U T-shirt that I was pretty sure he'd had since college. "Hardy little things. They take our spring frosts like champs."

"And they're yummy when Mom cooks them in sesame oil," I said with a smile. "Ready for dinner?"

"I sure am."

He followed me into the house, and we sat at the kitchen table to eat Mom's cheesy chicken and broccoli casserole. I came over for dinner once a week or so, usually stopping by after a hike like I had today. My phone rang about halfway through our meal. A quick glance showed that it was the Chittenden County Sheriff's Department, which meant they'd probably handled a situation that had left them with a pet that needed to be processed into the shelter.

"Sorry, I think it's work," I told my parents as I slipped into the living room to answer the call. "Hello?"

"Hi, Taylor, it's Laurie."

I'd gone to high school with Laurie, who was Deputy Laurie Siegel these days. "Hey, Laurie."

"Sorry to bother you after hours," Laurie said, "but we responded to a well check this evening and found the occupant of the home deceased. She had two dogs, and so far, it's looking like no one in the family wants to take them."

"I can meet you at the shelter in an hour," I told her.

"I appreciate it," she said. "And just so you know, we're pretty sure one of the dogs is pregnant."

3

PHOEBE

Downtown Burlington was busier than I remembered. As I walked through the pedestrian marketplace, I kept my head down, even though no one was looking at me. I'd come to Vermont to hide while I figured out how to pick up the pieces of my life, but after only twenty-four hours, my grandmother's cabin had begun to feel too quiet, too isolated. I was lonely, despite having FaceTimed with Courtney earlier today.

So here I was, wandering past shops and restaurants with no real idea of where I was headed. I'd just needed to get out of the house and out of my own head for a few hours.

A brightly painted rainbow in a nearby window caught my eye. The sign over the door read Vino and Veritas, Wine Bar and Bookstore, and suddenly, I was in the mood for a glass of wine. The pride flag in the window definitely helped to make my decision.

I opened the door and stepped inside, finding myself in an entranceway with a door to my right leading into the bookstore and the wine bar on my left. I entered the bar. The space was warm and inviting, with lots of wood and earth tones, and soft music played behind the buzz of conversation.

The bar area had several empty stools available, so I made my way to the closest one. I slid onto it and hung my purse on the hook beneath the counter. A pretty bartender with curly auburn hair approached.

"Hi," she said. "Know what you want?"

I hesitated, even though I knew she was asking about wine, but the truth was, I had no idea what I wanted anymore, not in this bar or anywhere else.

"We have a few specials this week, but whatever you're in the mood for, we probably have it." She pushed a leather-bound drink menu toward me with a friendly smile.

I glanced at it and then back at her. If I tried to peruse the wine menu on my own, the financial analyst in me would come out, crunching numbers as I compared flavors and ounces to price, and I'd spend half an hour choosing a glass of wine. "I'm over-whelmed just looking at that menu. What do you recommend?"

"You've got to give me something to go on," the redhead said, leaning her elbows on the counter. "Wine, beer, or cider?"

"Wine," I told her. "Something light and sweet…and not too expensive." As of last Friday, I was living out of my savings account, and while it would tide me over for a few weeks here in Burlington, it wouldn't last forever.

"I've got two specials you might like," she told me. "The first is a Late Harvest Chardonnay. It's crisp and sweet, with under-tones of orange peel and honeysuckle. The other is a prosecco rosé, fresh and bubbly with a hint of strawberry. And my favorite part…it's pink."

"How could I turn down a pink drink?" I said with a laugh. "I'll have a glass of that, please."

"You got it." The bartender turned away and reached into a small refrigerator beneath the counter. She pulled out a bottle and poured a glass of frothy pink wine, which she placed in front of me.

"Thank you." I sipped. The wine was sweet and bubbly on my tongue. If I closed my eyes, I could almost imagine I was in my favorite bar on Tremont Street in Boston. I could pretend I was still a financial analyst at Bern Finance, that Sabrina was still my girlfriend, that my life hadn't imploded. I could pretend that viral photo didn't exist.

"How's the rosé?"

My eyes popped open at the sound of the bartender's voice, and I blinked, grounding myself in this unfamiliar bar in Burlington, Vermont. "It's good. Thanks for the recommendation."

She gave me a thumbs-up before heading down the bar to check on her other customers.

I turned to face the room, watching the locals as they went about their Thursday evening. About half the booths in back were occupied, couples and groups of friends laughing and conversing over glasses of wine. Several of the tables in the middle of the room had been pushed together to accommodate a large group of young women who had a row of wine flights on trays between them. I envied their carefree attitude, laughing and drinking with friends. I'd been one of those girls until a few weeks ago.

And once, a very long time ago, I'd been a carefree teenager who loved Taylor Donovan with all my heart. I didn't think of Taylor often these days. Yes, I'd seen her at my grandma's funeral, but we hadn't spoken to each other. I hadn't talked to Taylor since I was sixteen. Seeing her yesterday had shaken me. It had reminded me of that one perfect summer we'd spent together.

Actually, I'd had a lot of happy summers with Taylor. Ever since I was a little girl, I'd spent my summers with my grandmother here in Vermont. Taylor's family lived just down the street, and she and I had quickly become best friends. Even then, she'd been an animal lover, always showing me baby birds and other wild creatures that she'd nursed back to health. In elementary school, she'd wanted to be a vet when she grew up, but later on, she'd decided she was too squeamish. I smiled to think of her working at the animal shelter now. Talk about finding the perfect job.

It made me wonder about my own job. Had I done as well as Taylor at following my dreams? I loved numbers and was an exceptional financial analyst, but did it make me as happy as saving homeless pets made Taylor? Suddenly, I wasn't sure.

As I sipped my wine, the carbonation tickled my tongue and stung my nose. Maybe I should have gotten the chardonnay. There was a small stage in the back corner of the bar with a piano tucked against the wall.

When we were kids, while Taylor was rescuing animals, I'd been playing my grandmother's piano and singing along to all my favorite songs. I hadn't played the piano in a decade.

"You have live music on the weekends?" I asked the bartender.

She nodded as she wiped down the counter. "Every Wednesday, Friday, and Saturday night. And we're hiring, if you know anyone who's interested."

I glanced at the piano. Maybe I should use my time here in Vermont to get back in touch with the things I used to enjoy. After all, when was the last time I'd done something just because it might be fun? "Actually...I'm interested."

TAYLOR

I walked down the row of dog kennels to check on our two newest arrivals, the dogs whose owner had passed away yesterday. Dexter was curled up on his bed in the back corner, but he got up and walked over when I approached his kennel. He was a pit bull, mostly white with a brown head and kind eyes, tail wagging hopefully.

"Hey, buddy," I said. "How are you today?"

His tail wagged faster, causing his whole body to sway from side to side.

"You're probably missing your mom, aren't you?" Today, I was hoping to locate a family member of his deceased owner who would step up to take him and Violet, the other dog that had been removed from the property last night.

Violet was going to be more difficult to place, though, if she was indeed pregnant. The vet would confirm when she arrived for rounds later today. I moved to stand in front of Violet's kennel. The brown pittie lay on her bed, fast asleep. Her belly was rounded, and her nipples were swollen. Her pregnancy was a foregone conclusion as far as I was concerned.

And that meant—unless a relative of her owner wanted to take her—I would have to find a foster home for Violet before she gave birth, because the shelter was no place for newborn puppies. I wished I could take Violet myself, but my lease agreement only allowed two dogs. Even if I moved Blue, my current foster, to a different home, my landlord would balk at the idea of puppies. But maybe a family member would come to claim the dogs. I had a list of people provided by the sheriff's department that I would be contacting today.

Violet lifted her head to look at me, and her tail began to wag.

"Hey, sweet girl," I said.

She got to her feet and approached the front of her kennel. Her tail was still wagging, but she trembled as she walked. She was scared, and for good reason. It must be terrifying to be uprooted from her home and placed in a concrete-walled kennel where she didn't know anyone, especially while she was pregnant.

"I'm going to get you out of here before those babies are born," I told her. I didn't reach through the bars to try to pet her. That was a great way to get my fingers bit. Not that I thought Violet was aggressive, but it was standard policy with any newcomer to the shelter. Frightened dogs were unpredictable. Instead, I crouched down to Violet's level and spoke softly to her.

As the care supervisor at the Chittenden County Animal Shelter, I oversaw the intake of new animals, coordinated the staff and volunteers who cared for them, and met with potential adopters to help them find the right pet for their family. Right now, my only full-time employee was Alleya, who would be coming through soon to walk the dogs and take Violet for her vet appointment, but we also had a number of volunteers who helped care for the animals.

I left Violet and spent a few minutes greeting the other dogs currently in our care before making my way back to my office. We were expecting five new cats on Monday, arriving through a transport program I'd helped to initiate that brought adoptable animals from overcrowded shelters in the South to find new homes here in Vermont. Thanks in part to my outreach efforts, the Chittenden County Animal Shelter was well funded and successfully placed hundreds of animals a year, including many that came to us from out of state.

Minnie leaped up to greet me as I entered my office, running in excited circles around me while Blue watched from his kennel in the corner. It was a huge job perk that I got to bring my dogs to work with me, although Minnie was endlessly miffed that she had to stay in my office while we were here.

"Let me make a few phone calls, and then I'll take you for that thing you want," I told her, not saying the word "walk" out loud so I didn't get her excited before I was ready. I sat at my desk and called the transport coordinator for the incoming cats. They'd be flying from Georgia into Boston, courtesy of a network of private pilots who volunteered their planes for animal rescue missions, and then a volunteer would drive them from Boston to Burlington.

Once I'd confirmed all the details, I opened the email the sheriff's department had sent me with a list of family members who might be able to take Dexter and Violet. First, I dialed the dead woman's sister, Jean, but the call rang through to voicemail. I made my way through the list, receiving one rejection after another. Just as I'd finished my last call, my phone rang.

"Chittenden County Animal Shelter, this is Taylor," I answered.

"Hi Taylor, this is Jean Templeton. You left a message earlier about my sister's dogs."

"Yes," I said, sitting up straighter in my seat. This woman was my last hope of getting Dexter and Violet out of the shelter today. "Thank you so much for getting back to me, and I'm so sorry for your loss."

"Thank you." Jean's voice trembled. "When we reach a certain age, we start to expect things like this, but I'm not sure anything ever truly prepares you."

"I can only imagine," I told her.

"It breaks my heart that Dexter and Violet have ended up at the shelter," Jean said. "Such wonderful dogs, both of them. After

I got your message, I talked it over with my husband, and we just don't think we can handle both of them. I hate to say it, but Alice was in over her head with those dogs, and especially with Violet turning up pregnant."

"It must have been a lot for her to handle," I agreed. As much as I wanted Jean to take them home, I also knew this wasn't a perfect match. Jean was elderly, and these dogs were young and energetic, not to mention the impending puppies.

"I can take Dexter," Jean told me. "He's a good boy, and I think I can manage him."

"Oh good," I said, glad at least one of them would go home with a relative. "And don't worry about Violet, Mrs. Templeton. I'll find a great home for her and her puppies."

"I hope so." I could hear the anguish in Jean's voice. "Will you let me know where she winds up? I'd like to know."

"I'll be sure to," I told her, making a note in Violet's file.

I spent several minutes making final arrangements for Jean to come in next week and pick up Dexter. Then I called my network of volunteers, putting out feelers for a foster home for Violet and asking for donations of puppy whelping supplies. We didn't get pregnant dogs in the shelter very often.

I took Minnie and Blue on a walk around the property and then returned to my office to spend what remained of the afternoon updating the shelter's social media. Around four, Alleya stopped by my office.

"Violet's definitely pregnant," she told me. "The vet saw at least four puppies on her X-ray and said they looked close to full-term. She could give birth as soon as next week."

"Oh boy," I said, rubbing the bridge of my nose. "I'd better step up my efforts to find her a foster home."

But when I left the office that evening, I was no closer to finding anyone to take her. I loaded Minnie and Blue into my SUV and drove home, thankful it was Friday. It had been a long week, and I was looking forward to a relaxing weekend with my dogs, although I let out a groan when I remembered I couldn't hike in my usual spot anymore. I'd tried not to let Phoebe occupy my thoughts these last two days and had been mostly successful, at least until now.

At home, I heated up a portion of the lasagna I'd made last weekend. Since I lived alone, I tended to cook once or twice a week and freeze portions for myself to eat the rest of the week. If I didn't, I'd eat prepackaged food all the time, and high blood pressure ran in my family, so I tried to watch my sodium intake.

After I ate, I took the dogs for a walk and went into my bedroom to change. Every Friday night, I went into town for a drink at Vino and Veritas. I changed into black jeans and a fitted tee, and then I applied some makeup, another Friday-night tradition. This was the only day of the week that I wore it.

I was content with my life the way it was, working at the shelter and fostering dogs, spending time with my family, and, hopefully soon, buying a home of my own. I'd love to add love to the mix, but it hadn't come my way yet, at least not since high school. Many of the women I met at V and V were just passing through, and while a fling could be fun, I wasn't interested in a long-distance relationship. Vermont was my home, and I never intended to leave. I wanted to fall in love with a local woman, and I didn't mind waiting for it to happen.

I put Blue in his crate before I left, while Minnie got the run of the apartment. Then I got into my SUV and drove to downtown Burlington. As I pushed through the door into the bar, I gave it a quick scan to see if I recognized anyone. There were a few regulars that I usually hung out with on Friday nights, but I didn't see any of them here at the moment.

I approached the bar, waving at the bartender, Rainn, who was pouring a glass of wine at the other end of the counter. He grinned at me, raising a finger to let me know he'd be right over. I settled myself on a stool and exhaled, letting the stress of the week slide off my shoulders, my unexpected reunion with Phoebe, the loss of the house I wanted to buy, and a heavily pregnant dog in need of a foster home.

For the next few hours, I was going to drink my favorite cider, listen to some live music, and hopefully enjoy the company of my friends. Maybe I'd even meet a woman here tonight. Who knew?

"How's it going?" Rainn asked as he set a glass of Shipley cider on the counter in front of me. For a while, he'd asked if I wanted my usual, and since I always did, he finally quit asking and just started bringing it. I was nothing if not a creature of habit.

"Not bad," I said. "You?"

"No complaints. Hang on." He patted the bar in front of me before making his way down to serve a group that had just come in.

I sipped my cider, savoring its tangy, refreshing flavor. Over the hum of conversation, I could hear a woman singing, accompanied by the tinkling notes of the piano. I stared into the amber depths of my cider while I enjoyed the soulful quality of the singer's voice. Whoever this was must be new, because I didn't recognize her voice or her style.

I picked up my glass and spun my stool toward the stage, only to find myself facing Phoebe. I inhaled, and my glass tipped dangerously in my hand. Of all the people I'd expected to see on that stage...

Phoebe's hair was pulled back in a loose bun, but a few dark curls had escaped to spill down her back. She wore a slinky black dress that highlighted her curves and stood out in stark contrast against her pale skin. Her voice was low and smoky, hitting me somewhere in the vicinity of my solar plexus, a jolt that warmed my stomach and radiated outward, flushing my skin.

As I watched, Phoebe looked up, and our eyes met. I lifted my glass and took another sip of my cider, feigning indifference, because it was just unfair that she could still affect me like this after so many years. Phoebe dropped her gaze to the piano in front of her as her fingers danced across the keys.

I remembered sitting beside her on the bench at Margery's piano, my arm wrapped around her as Phoebe sang. Her voice had been different then, lighter and sweeter, or maybe it just seemed that way, filtered through the blinds of my memory. Margery told me Phoebe had given up the piano—and singing— after she graduated from high school.

Maybe she was feeling nostalgic now that she was back in Vermont. Or maybe she was just trying to torture me with the allure of her voice. I gulped from my cider.

"Hi," a female voice said.

I spun to find myself facing an unfamiliar blonde. "Hi."

"I'm Rebecca. Are you from around here?"

"Taylor, and yes. You?"

"Just in town for the weekend," Rebecca told me.

"Ah." I sipped my cider. Rebecca was pretty, although not exactly my type with her trendy dress and long, red-painted nails. She looked like she'd never hiked a day in her life. But when I glanced to the left, I saw Phoebe watching me from the stage, and it gave me an absurd thrill to let her watch me flirt with someone else. "Where are you from, Rebecca?"

5

PHOEBE

I lowered my gaze to the sheet music in front of me. For the last hour, Taylor had been deep in conversation—a very flirty conversation, if looks were any indication—with a blonde at the bar. Was she Taylor's girlfriend? It was none of my business, of course. I didn't have feelings for Taylor anymore. I'd gotten over her years ago, and my heart was still bruised from losing Sabrina. Still, I was curious.

As I sang my way through a Taylor Swift favorite, I found my attention drifting to the other Taylor, watching her talk to the blonde. An off-key note twanged from the piano, refocusing my attention on the music. My piano skills were rusty at best, despite a day spent practicing on my Grandma's piano.

When the song ended, I heard a smattering of applause and even a few whistles from the bar's patrons. I wasn't sure whether they were just being polite, but at least they weren't booing me. Tanner Reid, the manager of Vino and Veritas, had given me a trial run tonight before making me a more permanent part of the lineup...or as permanent as I could be, given that I was only in town for a month or so.

Apparently, they were short musicians at the moment, so if tonight went well, I might have a recurring gig for as long as I was in Burlington. It could be just the distraction I needed while I was here. Sitting at this piano, singing some of my favorite songs, I felt something inside me come alive, the creative part of my soul that I'd buried deep beneath job and family obligations, number crunching, and a busy social calendar. The keys were smooth and solid beneath my fingers, familiar and comforting like an old friend.

I finished my set and stood, receiving another round of applause. The bar was a lot more crowded than it had been when I started playing, a fact I was glad I hadn't noticed until now. I smiled and thanked the people who'd been listening to me play, before making my way to the bar to check in with Tanner.

"Nice job tonight," he said. "You played well, and the crowd seemed to like you. I've got a couple of openings on the schedule over the next month or so that you could fill for us if you're interested. I'll email you with the details."

"Thank you," I told him. "I'd like that."

I rested an elbow on the bar, trying to decide whether to stay for a drink before I headed home. The stool beside Taylor was empty now. The blonde had either left or gone to talk to someone else. And that made my decision for me, because there were a few things I needed to say. I walked over to stand beside the empty stool. "Do you mind?"

Taylor turned to look at me, her eyes widening slightly. She gestured to the stool. "Go ahead."

I slid onto it and reached for a drink menu. I ordered a glass of chardonnay, then sat quietly as I waited for my drink to arrive. The bar around us buzzed with laughter and conversation, except for our little bubble of silence. I didn't want it to be this way between us. This was my fault, but hopefully, I could fix it.

Once I had my wine in hand, I took a fortifying sip. "I want to apologize for the way I handled our conversation on Wednesday. I wasn't expecting to see you, and I think I came off harsher than I intended."

"You think?" Taylor lifted her drink, shoulders tense. She had on snug-fitting jeans and a black T-shirt that hugged her curves. She had more of those than she did in high school, a woman's body, where before, she'd been a gangly teenager.

"You can still bring your dogs to hike on my grandma's land, at least until we start renting it out," I told her. "In fact, I hope you will. I'm sorry for being rude the other day."

"Okay," Taylor said, staring at her drink instead of at me. "Thank you."

"I guess I didn't know you and my grandma were so close." It had been bothering me since that afternoon. In fact, it was one of the reasons I'd been short with her. It had caught me off guard to realize Taylor still hiked here, that she'd been keeping up the property, that she'd even hoped to buy it.

"I'm surprised she never told you." Taylor did look at me then. The lighting in the bar caught her hazel eyes, making them dance with a myriad of colors.

"I am too," I admitted.

"She talked about you all the time."

I smiled into my wine. "I was her only granddaughter, after all."

"You didn't visit very often," Taylor said, and my smile fell flat.

"I came as often as I could, but my job kept me in Boston most of the time. After Grandma retired, she came down and stayed with my dad from Thanksgiving until Christmas every year, so I guess I saw her more in Massachusetts than here in Vermont."

"I just wondered," Taylor persisted, "why you're here for a month now but never managed it while she was still alive?"

"Forgot how nosy you are," I said, swirling my wine so that it caught the light.

Taylor laughed. "You got me. Some things never change."

"Well, if you must know, I lost my job last week...and my girl friend. So I decided to get out of town for a while."

"Damn," Taylor said. "I'm sorry."

"Thanks. I'm going to go out on a limb and assume you don't spend much time on social media."

"Busted," Taylor said. "Other than managing the accounts for the shelter, I don't really pay attention to it. Why?"

"Because I figured you would have recognized me if you were," I said.

"Recognized you from what?"

I pulled out my phone and opened the photo that had upended my life. In it, I stood in the middle of Lansdowne Street, hands raised and both middle fingers extended toward the man in front of me. Big block letters above my head said "ME," while "THE PATRIARCHY" was written above the man's head. I held my phone toward Taylor.

"Holy shit," she said. "Miss Prim and Proper flipped off a guy in the middle of Boston?"

"Well, he called me a bitch for not being impressed when he hit on me, so he had it coming," I told her.

"Asshole," Taylor said.

"Anyway, shit happens, but someone snapped this picture and captioned it, and it went viral all over social media. They call me 'girl against the patriarchy.'"

"Without your permission?" Taylor's eyebrows rose, amusement fading from her expression.

"Exactly. I'm not sorry for flipping him off, but all of a sudden, I was a viral meme for something that should have been a private moment. And unfortunately, my employer decided I was a liability to the firm."

"Oh shit. They fired you?"

I nodded, taking a large gulp of my wine.

"And your girlfriend? Did she break up with you because of the meme too?"

"You really *are* nosy," I said as an uncomfortable warmth crept up my neck and hurt radiated through my chest. "Yes. She got frustrated with all the unwanted attention."

"Phoebe, I'm sorry." Taylor rested a hand on mine. Her fingertips were cold where they'd touched her glass, yet somehow, they still spread warmth through my veins.

"Thank you."

"I could say something about running when things get tough, but I won't."

"I think you just did." I tugged my hand free from Taylor's. Damn, that hurt, and just when I was starting to think she and I could be friends again. "I was sixteen, Taylor, and so far in the closet, I didn't even know where the door was. I'm sorry I ran, okay?"

"I wasn't trying to push you out of the closet," she said. "But we were best friends. We emailed a million times a day, and then you just cut me off, like you forgot I existed."

"I didn't forget." My fingers clenched around the stem of my wineglass as unexpected tears pricked behind my eyes. "I never forgot."

Taylor lifted her glass and drank. "Could have fooled me."

6

TAYLOR

I loaded Blue and Minnie into the backseat of my SUV and set out for Margery's cabin. Well, Phoebe's cabin, at least for the time being. I was glad I'd get to hike here for a few more weeks, but that wasn't the only reason I'd agreed to come back. If I bumped into Phoebe while I was here, I was going to look for any and all opportunities to show her that this cabin was a home, not a rental property.

Maybe it wasn't too late. Maybe I could still change her mind. I loved this property in a way no renter ever could, and it wasn't as if her family needed the rental income.

I made the ten-minute drive to Mountain Laurel Road, pulling into the driveway behind Phoebe's purple Nissan. I swung my SUV to the side so I wasn't blocking her in. In the backseat, Minnie barked excitedly, bouncing from one end of the seat to the other while Blue attempted to stay out of her way.

"Come on, you two." I got out of the car and opened the back door for them. I clipped Blue's leash to his collar while Minnie trotted across the driveway, nose against the ground. Then her head came up, and she bounded toward the backyard. Before I'd realized what was happening, I heard Phoebe's startled exclamation. "Sorry," I called as I rounded the back of the house. "I didn't know you were outside."

"Minnie seems to have a habit of surprising me." Phoebe was crouched on the patio, rubbing Minnie behind her ears. She wore jean cutoffs and a pink-patterned tank top, and I really wished I wasn't affected by the sight of so much of her exposed skin, but it took real effort to keep myself from checking out her cleavage or the creamy expanse of her legs.

"She likes you," I said as Minnie flopped to the ground in front of Phoebe, begging for belly rubs.

"Well, I like her too."

"Sorry for busting in on you like this. Maybe I should start parking down the street." I'd always parked in the driveway, but it felt different now that Phoebe was living in the cabin. I felt almost like an intruder, and I didn't like it.

"No, it's fine. I don't mind." She stood, tugging at the hem of her shorts, which had ridden up, and again, I had to look away.

"Thanks. Well, we'll get out of your hair."

"Actually, do you mind if I tag along? I've been inside removing wallpaper all morning. I could use a little fresh air."

I hesitated. I *did* want the chance to talk to Phoebe about the cabin, but these hikes were my quiet time, a chance to bond with my dogs and with nature, and I was already concerned that my physical reaction to Phoebe meant my feelings for her weren't as dead as I'd hoped. "Sure, but you probably want to change your shoes." I gestured to her flip-flops.

"Okay," she said. "Give me just a minute to put on my sneakers."

I nodded, walking over to the rosebushes while I waited. I leaned toward the nearest bloom, closing my eyes as I inhaled its sweet scent. I'd always loved roses, probably at least partly because of Margery. They reminded me of afternoons here, helping Margery tend her garden and playing with her dog Comet in the backyard.

Hopefully, the Shaws would hire someone to tend the roses for their renters. I planned to suggest it, if I wasn't able to convince Phoebe to change her mind about renting the place out.

Minnie trotted over with a stick in her mouth, but she didn't drop it at my feet. She held on to it, staring hopefully at the back door of the cabin.

"Traitor," I told her, but Minnie was no dummy. She knew I would only throw the stick a few times, whereas Phoebe could potentially be coerced into humoring her for longer. Blue leaned in to sniff a rose, a boy after my own heart. He was a good dog, and once he'd come out of his shell, he'd make someone a wonderful pet. I had already seen him blossom in the week and a half he'd been with me.

The door opened, and Phoebe reappeared wearing aqua sneakers with pink laces. On cue, Minnie dropped the stick at her feet, bouncing in a circle as she barked at Phoebe.

"You're very subtle," Phoebe said with a laugh as she picked up the stick and gave it a toss.

Minnie dashed across the yard, pinning the stick to the ground with one front paw before she grabbed it in her mouth and trotted back to Phoebe.

"We should get going, or she'll have you standing here all afternoon, tossing that stick," I said.

"She reminds me a little bit of Comet." A wistful note crept into Phoebe's voice. "He was the same way with sticks."

"Yeah, he was." I led the way over the stream and onto the trail at the far side of the yard. "Have you hiked on these trails at all yet?"

She shook her head. "Not since we were kids."

"It's mostly the same," I told her. "I usually take the dogs to the field where—" I cut myself off as my brain caught up with my mouth. That field was where Phoebe and I had spent countless hours making out as teenagers. We would bring a blanket with us and hide from the world.

"Oh," Phoebe said quietly.

"But sometimes I cut through to the public trail to the west. It just means I have to put Minnie on leash."

"Let's do that," she suggested.

Yeah, I wasn't eager to return to the scene of our make-out sessions either. "Sounds like a plan. Minnie!" I called, realizing I'd lost sight of my dog.

There was a crash in the bushes, and Minnie's bushy black head appeared.

"What kind of dog is she?" Phoebe asked.

"She looks a lot like a Labradoodle, but she's a shelter dog, so I don't know for sure. She might just be a fuzzy mutt."

"She's definitely fuzzy," Phoebe agreed.

"You should see her when she's due for a trim," I said.

Phoebe smiled in that slightly lopsided way I'd always found so endearing. "I bet."

"Do you have any pets?" I asked.

She shook her head. "My condo in Boston doesn't allow them."

"Fair enough." I watched as Minnie dropped her stick at Phoebe's feet yet again. With a smile, Phoebe chucked it down the path ahead of us. "You're good with them, though."

"I like dogs," she said. The afternoon sun filtered through the trees overhead, casting dappled flecks of light over her skin.

I knew every step of this trail like the back of my hand. I knew every tree root and rock that bisected the path and every seasonal nuance to the scent of plants and earth along the way. But there was something new on the breeze today, a vaguely fruity fragrance that had to be Phoebe, her perfume or maybe her shampoo. Whatever it was, it was messing with my head.

Ahead, the trail curved sharply to the left. If we followed it, we'd wind up at the field. Instead, I waved a hand, indicating for Phoebe to follow me into the woods to our right. "If we cut through here, we'll come out on the public trail."

"You're sure you know where you're going?" she asked before shaking her head. "What am I saying? You've been hiking these woods your whole life. Lead the way."

"It's not far." I tromped over the leaf-strewn earth. "There's a scenic lookout up ahead, if you want to go that far."

"Sure," Phoebe agreed. She ducked beneath a low-hanging branch as Minnie trotted beside her.

I looked down at Blue, who walked quietly at my side. He was a quiet dog in general, anxious and withdrawn from whatever he'd gone through before he was surrendered to the shelter, but he looked relaxed out here in the woods, tongue out and tail up.

"Why does he stay on leash while Minnie runs loose?" Phoebe asked.

"Minnie's my dog. I've had her since she was a puppy and done extensive recall training with her, so I know I can let her run loose in the woods and she'll come when I call her," I told Phoebe. "Blue is my foster dog. He was only surrendered to the shelter a few weeks ago, and he's still extremely nervous."

"Aw," Phoebe said, giving the dog a sympathetic look.

"There's no telling how far he'd run if I let him off leash, and honestly, he probably feels more secure wearing it for now. He was so scared at the shelter, just shaking all the time, so I brought him home to help him get settled and gain the confidence he needs to go to a permanent home."

"Do you do that a lot?" she asked. "Bring dogs home from the shelter?"

"Yeah, I foster when I can, especially when we have a dog that could really blossom with a little extra care. My lease only allows me to have two dogs, though, so I can only foster one at the time since I have Minnie."

"Which is why you wanted to buy my grandma's cabin," Phoebe observed.

"One of the reasons."

There was a stream ahead, separating Margery's property

from the public land. Minnie leaped across it without hesitation, still with the stick in her mouth. "Stay, Minnie," I called, and she stopped, looking over her shoulder as she waited for us to catch up.

There were plenty of flat rocks in the stream that we could use to cross. Phoebe went first, sticking her arms out to the side for balance as she tiptoed from rock to rock. I followed, while Blue sloshed through the water, pausing for a drink. He slurped noisily, drawing a laugh from Phoebe.

I kept my eyes on him, ignoring the tug of yearning I felt at the sound of her laugh. It reminded me of afternoons just like this, afternoons when she and I explored these woods together, so caught up in each other, a bear could have walked right past us and we wouldn't have noticed.

On the other side of the stream, we joined up with the public hiking trail, and I directed Phoebe to the left. A few minutes later, we came to the scenic overlook. The Parks & Rec department had constructed a wooden gazebo where people could sit and look out at the mountains beyond.

"Oh, I remember this place," Phoebe said as she walked into the gazebo. "You and I used to come here sometimes. I never could find it on my own."

"Yeah, we did." I walked to the railing and looked out at the hilltops visible in the distance. "Sometimes I bring a book out here with me and just hide from the world."

"Sounds perfect."

"Not so different from why you're here in Vermont," I said.

"It's exactly why I'm here." Blue walked over to sniff her leg, and she sat on the bench to pet him. His tail wagged slowly at first, picking up speed as he relaxed into her touch. Phoebe looked up at me, eyes bright. "He likes me."

"Yeah, he does." I watched as she rubbed Blue behind his ears, talking softly to him. Soon the dog had rested his shoulder against her thigh, gazing up at her adoringly. "You're good with him."

"I've always liked dogs," she said. "I've just never had one of my own."

"Would you like to?" I asked, because an idea had just occurred to me, a way to get Violet out of the shelter before she gave birth. "I mean, just temporarily. Would you consider taking in a foster dog?"

"I don't know," Phoebe said, gazing at Blue. "Maybe if it was someone as quiet and sweet as Blue."

"I have a dog who needs to get out of the shelter ASAP, and I don't have any foster homes open to take her. She's very quiet and sweet. She's also very pregnant."

"Pregnant?" Phoebe's head popped up. "No way. I don't know the first thing about pregnant dogs...or puppies."

"I know. It's not ideal, but I'm at my wit's end trying to find someone who can take her, and I've got to get her out of the shelter before she gives birth. Even if you took her in temporarily, it would be a huge help."

"Why can't you take her?" she asked.

"Because my lease only allows two dogs."

Phoebe rubbed a hand down Blue's side. "What if I take him so you can foster the pregnant dog?"

I shook my head. "I can't have puppies. I've been over it with my landlord several times already over the years. She won't budge on it. It's one of the reasons I need my own place."

"I really can't, Taylor," Phoebe said. "I'm busy fixing up the cabin, and I'm leaving in a few weeks, not to mention puppies sound like a lot of work...and a lot of mess I don't need while I'm trying to get the place ready for renters."

Those were all good points, but I couldn't help feeling like this was somehow meant to be. "Just drop by on Monday and meet her?"

"It's not a good idea," Phoebe said.

"You're probably right, but it's the best idea I have at the moment."

"Taylor..."

"Stop by and meet her," I said, hoping I wasn't being too pushy, but I was desperate to get Violet out of the shelter. "That's all I'm asking."

She sighed. "I guess I could do that, but I'm not promising to take her home."

PHOEBE

I sat back on my heels to survey my work. This morning, I'd ripped up all the carpet in the living room, and that had been the easy part. My dad had offered to hire a contractor to install the laminate flooring he'd ordered, but I was trying to do things on my own for a change. I wasn't crazy about having a cabin full of contractors, but I might have to amend my opinion on that, because home renovations were a lot harder than I'd expected.

At any rate, I needed to get cleaned up and drive over to the animal shelter to meet the dog Taylor wanted me to foster. Bringing home a pregnant dog was a terrible idea, but maybe there was a different dog I could foster instead. Since I couldn't have pets in my condo in Boston, this might be my one chance to be a temporary dog owner.

I went down the hall to the guest bedroom, where the photo of me and Taylor as little girls still sat on the dresser. When we hiked together on Saturday, I was reminded of how close we used to be and how much I missed her, and now I found myself hoping we'd find a way to rekindle our friendship.

The circumstances behind my return to Vermont well and truly sucked, but maybe some good would come out of the trip too, the chance to make amends with Taylor, to rediscover my love of music, and to spend time in the places where I'd spent some of the happiest times of my childhood.

I went into the bathroom for a quick shower, then dressed in jeans and a yellow linen top. I put the address for the animal shelter into the GPS in my phone while I was still here in the cabin, allowing it to route my way while I was still connected to the Wi-Fi, as I'd been rudely reminded over the weekend that I didn't get much cell service up here.

Then I went outside and climbed into my car, blasting an upbeat playlist while I drove and singing along at the top of my lungs. Twenty minutes later, I pulled into the parking lot of a small white building. The sign in front read Chittenden County Animal Shelter.

"This is a mistake," I murmured as I shut off the car. Yeah, I loved dogs, and the idea of bringing one home to foster for a few weeks sounded kind of fun, but it was probably a lot more work than I had time for right now. The truth was, I wouldn't be here at all if I didn't feel I owed Taylor.

I walked to the front door and pulled it open, finding myself in a wood-paneled reception area. A corkboard to my left was covered with photos of dogs, cats, and other animals posing with the people I presumed had adopted them. There was no one behind the desk, so I went down the hall, easily finding Taylor's name on one of the doors. I tapped my knuckles against it.

"Come in," Taylor called.

I pushed the door open to find Taylor at her desk with glasses perched on her nose, giving her an adorably studious look. I only got a glimpse of her before Minnie came barreling toward me, barking happily as she planted her front paws on my jeans.

"Minnie, down," Taylor admonished, and the dog dropped to all fours, tail wagging as she looked up at me.

"I'm happy to see you too," I told her as I gave her a chin rub. "And you too, Blue," I said as I caught sight of the smaller dog in a crate in the corner. He lifted his head to look at me, quiet as ever.

"Thanks for coming," Taylor said as she took off her glasses and pushed back from the desk. She had on a black T-shirt with the shelter's logo on the front and gray jeans.

"Well, I'm not promising to foster the pregnant dog, but you might be able to convince me to take a lower-maintenance one," I told her. "And I'm glad to see the shelter anyway. I've never been here before."

"I'm pretty proud of it," Taylor said. "Jeri—the manager—and I have worked hard to make it as comfortable as possible for the animals who're waiting for homes and a positive experience for potential adopters. Want a quick tour?"

"I'd love one," I told her.

"Great, because I love giving them." She smiled at me as she led the way out of her office, closing the door behind her to keep her dogs inside.

I glimpsed Minnie's tragic expression as the door closed in her face. "I think you just broke her heart."

"She's dramatic," Taylor said, rolling her eyes playfully. "But she can't come into any of the areas where the adoptable pets are. It gets them all worked up." She led the way back through the lobby to a door on the other side. When she opened it, a loud meow echoed through the room. "That'll be Oscar. He likes attention."

I found myself facing a glass wall, through which I could see various cat perches and even an oversized armchair, currently occupied by an orange cat who was watching us intently. Taylor opened a glass door and let us into the cat enclosure. I counted about ten cats inside, all different sizes and colors.

"Do they all get along?" I asked.

"Right now, they do," Taylor told me. "When we have someone who doesn't like to hang out with the group, we have a couple of individual enclosures we can set up in the lobby so they can be the only cat in their space."

"How long have these guys been here?" I asked as the orange

cat walked over to rub himself against my legs. I bent to pet him, and he immediately started purring.

"That's Oscar. He's only been here since last week, and I don't imagine he'll stay long, for obvious reasons." Taylor gave him an affectionate look as he pressed his head against my hand for a more vigorous chin rub. "Some of them have been here a few months or longer. And I've got five cats quarantined in back who just arrived from Georgia."

"Georgia?" I asked. That seemed like an awfully long way for cats to travel to a shelter.

"There are a lot of overcrowded shelters in the South," Taylor told me. "So I arrange to have adoptable animals transported here whenever we have space. It's a win-win, because it frees up some much-needed space in overworked shelters, while it keeps my kennels full. Without our transport program, I would some-times have more people looking to adopt than I do adoptable pets."

"Wow, I had no idea."

Taylor let us out of the cat enclosure and led the way into the next room, where a row of smaller cages had been lined up against the wall. "This is where our small animals stay. Right now, we have a pair of guinea pigs, but we also get a lot of rabbits and sometimes hamsters and mice too."

"Aw, look at them." I peered into the first cage, where a pair of black-and-white guinea pigs sat munching on hay.

"Their names are Cookie and Cupcake."

"Cute." I followed her through another door, which led into a long, narrow hallway that immediately filled with a combination of barking, whines, and the clang of paws against the metal bars at the front of the kennels.

"Give them a second, and they'll settle down," Taylor said. "It's almost time for Alleya to come through for their afternoon walk, so they're excited."

"Aw, this one looks so sad," I said as I caught sight of a small dog with big ears looking up at me from the first kennel.

"That's Lola. Her owner gave her up a few weeks ago because her new boyfriend is allergic to dogs."

"Oh shit," I said. "That's terrible."

"It is, but we'll find her a new home soon. The girl I want to introduce you to is at the end of the hall." Taylor motioned for me to follow.

"Doesn't Lola need a foster home?" I asked as we walked. "She's small and seems quiet. I could see having her around for a few weeks."

"She could benefit from a foster home," Taylor said. "But she's also extremely adoptable for the reasons you said—plus she's adorable—so I'm hopeful we'll be able to place her quickly, especially since she's the first face potential adopters see when they come through the door."

"It sure worked on me," I said.

"These two came in last Wednesday," Taylor told me. "Their owner passed away unexpectedly. Her sister is stopping by tomorrow to pick up Dexter, the male dog, but she didn't feel comfortable taking both, especially since Violet's about to give birth."

"Yeah, that part is what's giving me pause too," I said.

"Believe me, if I had anyone else I could send her home with, I would." Taylor stopped in front of the last kennel in the room. A brown dog with a wide face and a round, stocky body stared up at us. There was a white stripe running down her face, ending just above her nose.

"Oh," I said, taking an involuntary step backward. "Is she a pit bull?"

"She is," Taylor said, "but I promise you that's not a bad thing."

"Sorry," I said. "But they're used in dog fights, aren't they? I've heard they're aggressive."

"They can be, but so can most breeds." Taylor's expression was neutral, but I knew her well enough to see her disappointment over my reaction to Violet's breed. "They get a bad rap in the news, but this girl has already passed a rigorous behavioral assessment. She didn't display any signs of aggression toward humans or other dogs, and she was a loving companion to an elderly woman until a few days ago."

"But she's still about to give birth to a litter of puppies, which I know absolutely nothing about." I didn't like anything about the idea of bringing Violet home. Lola, on the other hand…

"Let's take her for a walk so you can get to know her a little better," Taylor suggested, as stubborn as she was beautiful.

"All right, but for the record, I still think this is a bad idea." I glanced into the kennel beside Violet's, where another pit bull—this one white with brown markings—stared back at me, tail wagging. "Is he Violet's baby daddy?"

Taylor laughed. "No, he's actually her brother. He was neutered, but their owner couldn't afford Violet's spay. She also didn't always keep Violet on leash, and she apparently wandered off and got herself pregnant."

"Hm." I watched with apprehension as Taylor opened the front of the kennel. She rubbed the dog and spoke gently to her before attaching Violet's leash.

"Here you go," Taylor said, holding the leash out to me.

I grasped it, but as I looked down at the dog, I was wishing I'd stayed home today. I could have already started putting down the new flooring—or given in and hired a contractor to do it for me. Violet walked out of her kennel, gazing up at me with brown eyes that appeared slightly too small for her face. Her tail gave a hesitant wag, as if she wasn't any more enthusiastic about this walk than I was. Her belly was indeed swollen, but maybe not as much as I would have anticipated for a pregnant dog.

Taylor led the way down the hall, while Violet walked at my side. We went out a door that led onto the shelter's grassy side yard, and Violet immediately squatted to pee.

"Just like a pregnant lady," I said.

"Yep," Taylor agreed. "She eats a lot too. I'll go over all her care with you if you decide to foster her."

"If," I repeated.

"It's really not as hard as you're probably thinking," Taylor said. "Violet will do all the hard work, and I can have someone come over and help when she goes into labor. We have several volunteers who're experienced with whelping puppies."

"I don't even know what whelping is," I protested.

"It's just a fancy word for a dog giving birth," Taylor explained.

"If you have experienced volunteers, why doesn't one of them take her, then?"

"One of them has an elderly dog who's gotten grumpy in her old age and doesn't like other dogs in the house, and the other has a new baby of her own. Neither of them is fostering at the moment, but they could definitely give you a helping hand."

I pressed my lips together. I could see where Taylor was coming from. Surely it was better for Violet to give birth in an inexperienced foster home than at the shelter, but I had my own life to think about. I needed to focus on getting the cabin renovated so I could go back to Boston, which didn't leave much time for a dog, not to mention that the puppies would pee all over my brand-new floors and probably chew on stuff too.

"How long do puppies stay with their mother?" I asked.

"About eight weeks."

"Taylor...I'm not going to be here that long."

"Then I'll move them when you need to leave," she said. "Right now, I'm just focused on getting her out of the shelter before she gives birth. Ideally, I'd like her to stay in one home until the puppies are weaned, but as an animal rescuer, I don't always deal with ideal situations. Sometimes, you just have to make the best of what you have available."

I looked down at the dog. Violet stared right back, and when we made eye contact, I felt a tug in my chest. She really did have a sweet face, and she seemed mellow and well-behaved. Was I really thinking about this? "Is she housebroken?"

"Yes. Her owner's sister says Violet is a perfect lady in the house, no bad habits that she was aware of, although she does have a penchant for chasing squirrels, so you want to make sure to keep her on leash in the yard."

"Doubt she's doing much squirrel chasing at the moment," I said.

Indeed, Violet plodded along, belly swaying from side to side. Her tail hung limply behind her, and I didn't know much about dogs, but it seemed sad somehow, like it should be up and wagging if she were happy.

"This must be confusing for her," I said. "Losing her owner and coming to the shelter."

"Definitely," Taylor agreed. "Want to sit on that bench over there for a few minutes?"

"Sure." I walked toward it with Violet at my side. When Taylor and I sat, Violet lay down on the grass in front of us, but she still didn't seem relaxed. Her head was up, and her eyes were alert, watching us. "She's very vigilant."

"Because she's not comfortable here, and her instincts are telling her she needs to find a safe place for her puppies."

"Dammit," I muttered. It was working. I was starting to go soft for the dog. When I stared into Violet's eyes, I felt a connection I hadn't expected.

"Is that a good 'dammit'?" Taylor asked.

"Good for *you*...maybe." I couldn't seem to look away from Violet, who was staring back at me with the same intensity. "She has very expressive eyes."

"She does," Taylor agreed.

"I hate that she looks so worried."

"The sooner she gets out of here, the better, so she'll have time to get settled and start to feel relaxed in her foster home before the puppies come."

I slid off the bench to sit on my knees in the grass in front of Violet. "What do you think? I'm not sure if you want to give birth while I'm putting down laminate floors."

Violet's tail thumped against the grass as she leaned forward to sniff my arm.

"You're redoing the floors?" Taylor asked.

I nodded. "The carpet was old and worn and smelled like dogs."

"I didn't realize you were doing so much work on the place."

When I looked over my shoulder, Taylor was frowning. "Having second thoughts about wanting me to take her home?"

"It's not ideal, especially if you have contractors coming in and out."

"That's what I've been trying to tell you." I rubbed Violet under her chin, and her tail thumped the grass again. "I'm trying to put down the laminate on my own, since I'm not wild about a house full of contractors either, but I'm not sure how well it'll go."

"What if I come over and help?" she offered.

"Really?"

Taylor looked at Violet and then at me. "I'm asking a huge favor of you, so if you take her, I'll do what I can to return the favor. I was already going to offer to help with her, but I could probably nail some floorboards too."

"I'll think about it," I told her.

Taylor pressed her lips together. "We don't have much time for you to decide."

"I'm sorry, but I don't like to make big decisions on the spot. I need to make sure I've thought through all the risks." It was the financial analyst in me. Sometimes I just couldn't turn her off.

"Fine," Taylor said, sounding resigned. She knew as well as I did that if I walked out of this shelter without Violet, I probably wasn't coming back for her. But I just couldn't commit to this, not right now. It was too much.

We went inside and put Violet back in her kennel. When the door clanged shut behind her, Violet's whole demeanor changed. Her eyes seemed to dull, and her tail drooped. She trudged to the bed in her kennel and curled up on it, facing the wall like she'd accepted that she was never getting out of here.

And my heart broke. "All right, I'll take her, but just for a few weeks until you find a more qualified foster home."

Taylor beamed at me. "Really?"

I nodded, swallowing hard. "I can't...I can't leave her here to have her babies in jail."

"Thank you," she said quietly. "I really appreciate this."

I looked at Violet, and my stomach twisted uncomfortably. What had I gotten myself into? "So what happens next?"

"I have some paperwork for you to fill out before you take her home," Taylor said.

"You want me to take her right now?"

"I mean, you don't have to, but I think it's best. I could send her home with you now, and then stop by your house after I get off work to help you get her settled?"

"Okay, I guess." One good thing to come out of this might be the chance to spend more time with Taylor. Maybe this dog would help us repair our friendship. After all, we'd only been lovers for one secret summer when we were sixteen, but we'd been best friends since we were seven, and maybe we could be again.

In her office, I filled out several forms while Taylor explained that she was able to fast-track me as a foster home since we already knew each other. Then she handed me pamphlets and other information to take home with me.

"You're only responsible for buying her food, although I'll send you home with a bag to get you started. We pay for all the veterinary care for her and her puppies," Taylor told me.

"How do I know how to care for her? Or when she's going into labor?"

"The paperwork I just gave you covers a lot of it," she said. "But I'll stop by and go over everything with you in more detail once I'm finished here. I have an approved adopter coming by in about a half an hour, and another appointment after that, but I'll come by after, okay?"

"What about other supplies? A bed and all that stuff?" I asked.

Taylor stood from behind her desk. "I've got you covered. I

put out a call to my volunteers on Friday when I realized I was going to have to look outside my usual network of foster homes for Violet, and they've brought in everything you'll need."

I went down the hall with her, and we soon had my car loaded with food, bowls, and a bed, with Taylor promising to bring more supplies with her later, because we had to save room on the backseat for Violet herself. As I looked at the items piled in my trunk, I felt a flash of panic. What the hell was I doing?

My panic had only grown by the time I led Violet out the shelter's front door ten minutes later. This was probably going to be disastrous, for me, for Violet, for the puppies, and for the cabin I was supposed to be renovating.

I opened the back door of my SUV, gesturing for Violet to hop in, hoping she knew what to do because I was afraid to reach under her stomach and lift her since she was pregnant. She looked at the car and then at me, and her tail gave an actual wag. Then she hopped in and curled up on my backseat like she'd done it a million times before.

"Look at that," Taylor said from behind me. "She knows you just sprung her from jail."

"How?"

"They always know, and she won't forget it."

TAYLOR

It was almost six by the time I turned my SUV into the driveway behind Phoebe's purple Nissan. I walked up the path to the front door and knocked, hoping she and Violet were off to a good start together. It certainly wasn't an ideal situation, but it had been the best I could come up with on such short notice, and my gut instinct said Phoebe would rise to the occasion.

The door swung open, and Phoebe stood there, wearing the same jeans and yellow top she'd had on at the shelter earlier. Her hair was down now, loose curls spilling over her shoulders. I'd always had a weakness for her curls. I had to resist the urge to reach out and coil one of them around my finger the way I'd done that magical summer.

"Hi," I said instead. "Everything going okay?"

She nodded, motioning me inside. "So far, she just follows me around the house and watches me. If I want her to lie in her bed, I have to sit down too."

"That's fine. She'll start to settle down soon." I followed Phoebe into the living room, which was currently stripped to the plywood beneath the carpet. Violet walked ahead of us and lay on the blue corduroy bed I had sent home for her.

"I'm worried," Phoebe admitted, hands twisting in front of

her. "I have no idea what I'm doing. I keep looking at her to make sure she hasn't quietly given birth over there without me noticing."

"The vet thinks she has about a week to go," I told her. "But I'll go over all the signs of labor to look for while I'm here. We also need to build her a whelping area. It would be a good idea for her to start sleeping there at night right away, so she gets comfortable in it."

Phoebe's eyes widened. "What's a whelping area?"

"It's where she's going to give birth. What room do you plan to have her sleep in?"

"I don't know. Mine, I guess?"

"The master bedroom?" I asked.

She shook her head. "I haven't gone in there yet. The guest room is where I've always stayed when I'm here."

"It's too small for you and Violet and a whelping box full of puppies, though," I said. Margery's guest room was barely larger than the twin-sized bed and dresser that resided in it.

Phoebe took a deep breath, reaching up to fidget with one of her curls. "I guess I've been a little afraid to go in her bedroom. I mean, she died in there." Her voice was soft, and she dropped her gaze to her hands.

I had an unexpected urge to hug her. "Would it help if I went in with you?"

She gave me a tight smile. "I have to go in sooner or later, right? Let's just do it."

"Sure," I agreed.

She stood and led the way down the hall, pausing in front of the guest room. "You're sure it's too small?"

I peered over her shoulder, unprepared for the rush of nostalgia I felt when my gaze fell on the blue-striped quilt. How many hours had Phoebe and I spent in this room? As girls, we'd played with our dolls or raced my Hot Wheels around on the floor. Later on, we'd laid on the bed together, sharing teen drama while Phoebe talked about which boys she liked.

I'd been sitting on that bed when I told Phoebe I wasn't sure I liked boys.

And when we shared our first kiss.

My heart thumped against my ribs at the memory of Phoebe's lips, sticky and sweet like the strawberry lip gloss she'd been so fond of that summer. I remembered the wonder in her eyes after that kiss, as if the world had shifted beneath her. I liked to think that it had.

Present-day Phoebe turned to face me, and we were standing way too close. Her gaze darted to my lips as if she'd been thinking about the same thing, and I took a quick step backward. I wasn't going there with her, not again. She'd panicked and run the first time, and she'd do it again, if for no other reason than the fact that she was only here for a few weeks.

"It *is* small in here," she said, her gaze darting to the bed and back to me. Every spare inch was currently occupied by the elephant in the room, and that elephant was getting bigger by the moment.

"Let's look at your grandmother's room," I suggested.

She brushed past me and opened the door at the end of the hall, then turned to the side as if she couldn't quite bear to look inside. I stepped up behind her, resting a hand on her shoulder as I looked around the room. I'd never been in Margery's bedroom before. I'd only glimpsed it on my way to the bathroom in the hall. It was large, with a full-sized bed in the center and a variety of heavy wooden furniture against the walls, which were covered in rose-printed wallpaper.

The bed was neatly made, and the room—though slightly stuffy from having been closed up for so long—gave no indication that anyone had died here.

"You okay?" I asked her.

Phoebe nodded, walking farther into the room. "I don't know what I was expecting, but it feels the same as always, like she's just gone out to run an errand or something."

"That corner would be perfect for a whelping box," I said,

pointing. "I'd ordinarily hesitate to suggest whelping puppies in your grandma's bedroom, but I know Margery wouldn't mind. In fact, she'd probably have done it herself if she were still here."

When Phoebe turned to face me, her eyes were suspiciously glossy. "Yeah, I guess she would have. So, I'll put the box in here, but what is it, exactly?"

"Well, what I have for you isn't actually a box. We're on a budget here, so I've got a child's playpen that we're going to put some comfortable blankets in for her to make a nice nest for herself. When it gets closer, we'll put absorbent pads in there for her to give birth on."

Phoebe pressed her lips together as she stared at the corner in question. "Let's do it, then."

We went out to my car to get the supplies and spent the next fifteen minutes putting together the plastic playpen and filling it with bedding. I left the baby gate open so Violet could come and go as she wished for the time being. She'd watched the whole process with interest, and now she poked her head into the enclosure.

"You like that, Violet?" Phoebe asked, patting the blanket. "It's for you."

Violet walked inside the pen and sniffed at the bedding, then whined.

"Oh no," Phoebe said. "She doesn't like it."

"She'll be fine," I said, hoping it was true. I didn't have much puppy experience myself, and dogs sometimes had their own opinions on where they wanted to give birth. "I'll have Holly and Peyton—my volunteers with puppy whelping experience—stop by this week to offer their expertise."

Violet pawed at the bedding, shuffling it around inside the pen, then nipped at it.

"She's chewing it up." Phoebe sat back on her heels, frowning as she brushed a curl out of her eyes.

"Or she's trying to get it how she wants it," I said. "And if she doesn't like this blanket, we'll give her a different one to try."

"I can't believe I let you talk me into bringing home a pregnant dog."

"I can't believe you did either," I teased, trying to keep the mood light. Truthfully, I had no idea if this foster situation would work out, but I was hopeful. "And speaking of bedding, do you want to swap out what's on the bed before you sleep in here tonight?"

Phoebe's head bowed. She let out a slow breath, and then she nodded.

We went through the closet to find clean sheets and blankets and remade the bed so it would be new for her. "There," I said as I smoothed out the quilt. "A fresh start."

She looked at me, eyes brimming with emotion. "I'd definitely like one of those."

9

PHOEBE

I blinked at the unfamiliar ceiling with bleary eyes before rolling to my side to look in Violet's playpen. It was empty. Last night had been a disaster. Violet had whined and cried when I tried to close her inside the pen, but every time I opened the gate, she promptly got out and started wandering the house. Consequently, neither of us had gotten much sleep, and I had half a mind to call Taylor and ask her to take the dog back to the shelter.

But then I remembered the look on Violet's face when she'd been in her kennel there, the resignation in her eyes. Surely I could give this another day to try to make it work. But first, I had to find Violet and hope she hadn't destroyed anything or peed all over the exposed particle board in the living room, or worse... delivered puppies in a random corner of the house.

I climbed out of bed and tugged a sweatshirt over my tank top. I bypassed the master bathroom in favor of the guest bath in the hall where all my things were. It had been weird sleeping in my grandmother's room last night. I'd thought it might be depressing or even creepy, but oddly, I'd felt closer to her there, almost like I could feel her presence in the room. It might have been comforting if I'd actually gotten the chance to rest instead of chasing after Violet all night.

I freshened up and went down the hall, where Violet was curled in a tight ball on the dog bed in the living room. "You didn't have puppies out here by yourself, did you?"

She raised her head and stared at me. She didn't look happy, but I didn't see any puppies, at least, or any obvious signs that she'd gotten into trouble out here by herself.

"I bet you're ready to go out." I picked up the leash on the kitchen counter.

Violet got to her feet, and she was definitely still pregnant, thank goodness. I clipped the leash onto her collar and led the way out the back door. She squatted to do her business, and then I led her around the perimeter of the backyard for good measure.

"If this is going to work, you and I are going to have to get to know each other, I think," I told her. "I'm guessing if you weren't pregnant, you'd enjoy a nice hike in the woods the way Taylor does with her dogs."

Violet cocked her head to the side, staring at me.

"But maybe what you actually want right now is breakfast. Actually, so do I. And coffee, but that's just for me." I wasn't sure why I was talking out loud to her, but she seemed like she might like it. She watched me closely every time I spoke to her.

What was I going to do with her? Last night hadn't gone well, and I couldn't shake the feeling that she wasn't happy here. We went back inside, and I took off her leash before walking to the instructions Taylor had left for me. Violet would get a mixture of wet and dry food, the same as she had for dinner last night. "I do think it's funny that you eat puppy chow," I told her as I popped open a can and began to mix it all together. According to Taylor, Violet needed the extra calories.

I put the bowl on the floor and turned my attention to my own breakfast. I flipped on the coffee machine and popped a bagel in the toaster. My phone chimed with an incoming text message.

How did her first night go?

It was from Taylor, of course. And I shouldn't feel a thrill at the sight of her name, because she was only inquiring about the dog.

Rough. She hates the pen we made her, I replied.

I have an idea for that. I'll stop by after work, if that's okay.

Sure.

Call me if you have any questions today.

I put my phone down, frustration rising in my chest as I looked at the living room, which was completely torn apart. I had so much work to do here, and I had a feeling I wasn't going to get anything done today but worry about Violet.

I spread jam onto my bagel, poured myself a mug of coffee, and sat at the kitchen table. I had no idea what to do with a dog all day. My grandma had always had a dog around, but I couldn't remember what Comet *did* all day. Sleep? Chew on a bone? Maybe I should give Violet some toys to play with.

"You don't look like you'd play with toys," I told her before biting into my bagel. On the contrary, Violet might be the most serious dog I'd ever met. If she were a person, I was sure she'd never smile.

Right now, she lay with her head between her front paws, watching me eat my breakfast now that she'd finished her own. Maybe she'd like to watch me do some work around the house later too. But first, we sat and stared at each other while I finished my bagel and coffee. It was unnerving. She didn't seem to blink very often.

To distract myself, I picked up my phone and started thumbing through my notifications. My friend Courtney had texted to ask how things were going in Vermont and to let me know #girlagainstthepatriarchy had finally stopped trending on Twitter. I had deleted the app from my phone before I left Boston. I'd been proud of the photo for a hot second before it destroyed my life. Now I never wanted to see it again.

When you get back to Boston, we should talk.

The text appeared on my screen without warning, and I stared at it for a moment in shocked silence. It was from Sabrina, the first time I'd heard from her since she walked out on me two weeks ago.

Yes was the first word that came to mind. I wanted to reply that I'd be happy to meet her whenever and wherever she wanted, because maybe she'd had a change of heart. Maybe she realized she'd made a mistake.

But as I began to text her back, tears filled my eyes. *Dammit.* What could Sabrina possibly say to make this right? How could I ever trust her again? The truth was, I hadn't spent nearly as much time here in Vermont pining over her as I'd thought I would. I was lonely, sure. But I had a sneaking suspicion that I was missing the rest of my friends and family in Boston more than I was missing Sabrina.

Tears spilled over my cheeks, and I wiped them away as I finished my coffee. On the dog bed, Violet whined.

"It's okay," I told her. "People cry sometimes. Didn't your owner ever cry, or was she one of those eternally happy people?"

Violet just stared.

"Well, I cry," I said. "Sometimes, I cry a lot, because I miss my friends and my condo in Boston. I had a whole life there, you know? And some random asshole took a picture of me without my permission and ruined my life with it."

Silence from the dog bed.

"Anyway, if you and I are going to sleep in my grandma's old bedroom, we need to pack up her things and make it ours. Hopefully, you'll like it better tonight than you did last night." I picked up my phone and deleted my half-formed response to Sabrina. She didn't deserve a reply, at least not yet. For all I knew, she just wanted to ask for that sweatshirt of hers that I'd found in the laundry last week.

"All right, you," I said to the dog. "Let's go pack up my grandma's bedroom."

TAYLOR

I pulled into Phoebe's driveway and parked in my usual spot behind the purple Nissan. I wasn't sure when I'd started thinking of this as Phoebe's driveway, though, because it wasn't. Phoebe had never lived here. She'd visited as a child, and she was visiting now. And I needed to remember that distinction.

"I'll be right back, you two," I told the dogs in the backseat. "I just have something to give Phoebe, and then we'll go on our hike."

I cracked the windows before I shut off the car, laughing at the horrified look on Minnie's face as she realized I was leaving her behind. This wasn't part of our routine. Minnie had always been welcome at Margery's house, but Violet needed time to settle in, which meant not introducing her to any new dogs at the moment.

I carried a stack of blankets and towels with me as I walked toward the front door, but when I knocked, there was no answer. Phoebe's car was in the driveway, though, so she must be around somewhere. I knocked again, peering through the window, but I couldn't see any sign of her or Violet inside.

I turned around to find Minnie with her fluffy nose stuck through the crack in the window, watching. "You're ridiculous, you know that? I'll be right back."

I walked around behind the house, and the sight that greeted me sent a warm zing through my system. Phoebe lay on her stomach on a pink blanket beneath Margery's rosebushes with her feet kicked up behind her and a paperback in her hands. Violet lay on the blanket beside her, fast asleep in the sunshine.

I pressed a hand against my chest, because *oof*, my heart. There was nothing sexier to me than a woman with a dog, and this woman with this dog had just put a serious dent in the armor I'd spent so many years strengthening. I couldn't fall for Phoebe again, not unless I wanted to get my heart broken a second time.

I cleared my throat. "Hey."

Phoebe looked over her shoulder with a smile as the sun cast golden highlights through her brown curls. "Hi."

"I brought some new bedding for you to try in Violet's whelping box."

"Good, because she hates everything I've put in there so far," Phoebe said as she rolled over and sat up, leaving her book face down on the blanket to keep her place. "But what makes you think she'll like these blankets better?"

"Because they came from her owner's house."

"Oh," she said. "That's sweet...or morbid, depending."

"Comforting is what I was going for," I said. "Hopefully, they'll smell like home to her."

"It's certainly worth a shot, but...are they clean? Because you've just brought me a dead woman's blankets."

I laughed. "Yes. These things all came out of her linen closet."

"How did you get them?"

"Her sister came to the shelter to pick up Dexter today, so I asked her to bring a few things that smelled like home for Violet."

"That was good thinking. I hope she likes them."

"Me too. Want me to set them inside for you? I left my dogs in the car, so I need to go get them."

"Sure," she said. "You're on your way out for a hike?"

"Yeah. I didn't want to stress Violet out by introducing them." I opened the back door and stepped inside, frowning at the exposed particle board. I'd told Phoebe I'd help her lay new floors if she fostered Violet, and I needed to make good on that promise. I crossed to the kitchen table and left the bedding there before walking back outside. "Still need help with the floors?"

She nodded. "If you don't mind. I didn't get much done at all today with Violet underfoot. I keep worrying she's going to sneak off and have puppies somewhere."

"I can come by after work tomorrow and help for a few hours if that's a good time for you," I offered.

"That would be great. Thank you."

Violet got to her feet and walked to me, tail wagging shyly. Her leash dragged behind her in the grass.

I crouched to pet her. "Contrary to what you might think, she seems like she's doing really well here so far. She's restless and unsettled with everything that's happened, and her hormones are telling her to start getting ready for the puppies, but she seems to feel comfortable with you."

"Well, I hope so," Phoebe said. "But I still think she'd be better off somewhere else."

"She likes you, Phoebe. Just look at her."

Violet walked back to the blanket and plopped down beside Phoebe, tail wagging. Phoebe gave her a hesitant smile. "I can't stop worrying about her."

"Try not to. You'll only stress her out. Chances are she'll deliver the puppies just fine with minimal help from you. Animals are pretty good at this stuff."

"And if she doesn't?"

"I'll make sure someone's here with you to help," I told her. "And in the meantime, I'll be back tomorrow without my dogs so I can help you with those floors."

PHOEBE

"We need to get some sleep tonight, Violet," I said. "Both of us, okay?"

She looked at me with those soulful brown eyes. There was nothing flat or dull about Violet's eyes. They showed everything she was feeling, and right now, they looked anxious.

"Taylor brought you a new blanket. It was your owner's. Let's see if you like it." I patted the inside of the playpen, where I'd arranged the new blanket on top of one of my grandma's.

Violet leaned through the open gate and sniffed, and then her tail started to wag. She walked all the way into the pen and pawed at the blanket, but this seemed less hostile than the way she'd pawed at it last night and more like she was trying to get comfortable. She nipped the blanket, and then she began to spin. She tugged and pawed and spun until I was dizzy just watching her, and then she plopped down in the middle of the bedding, looking up at me as her tail thumped the bed.

"You like that?" I asked.

Violet's tail thumped again.

I took that as a yes. Thank *God*. I shut off the light, beyond exhausted after last night. To my relief, there was silence in the playpen. Violet seemed ready to crash tonight too. As I drifted to sleep, my last thought was of Taylor, spouting dog knowledge from those soft pink lips, the first lips I had ever kissed.

When I woke the next morning, Taylor's face still lingered in my mind with a hazy kind of familiarity, as if I'd spent most of the night dreaming about her. Not only that, but the ache between my thighs suggested they might have been sexy dreams. I wished I could remember them. Our summer together had been so long ago, and we'd kept it such a secret that sometimes it felt more like a fairy tale than something that had actually happened.

I'd been so young and inexperienced at sixteen. It had never even occurred to me that I might like girls. I'd been so focused on boys because that was all my other friends talked about. And then there was Taylor, quietly confident as she told me she was gay. And more than that, she'd already had her first girlfriend, another girl in her class.

I'd been floored by the revelation, had felt naïve by comparison. I'd never even thought about kissing a girl, and suddenly, it was *all* I could think about. And not just any girl. I'd started daydreaming about kissing Taylor. I had romantic notions about us being more than friends, soulmates, even. Just like that, my best friend had become the only person I could imagine myself being with, the only person I wanted to kiss.

It didn't happen for several long, dramatic weeks, afternoons filled with unnecessary touching and near misses as we fumbled our way toward our first kiss. We'd been sitting side by side on my bed, right here in this house, looking at something on my laptop, when we both turned our heads and our lips collided.

Something came to life inside me that I'd never felt before, a heat and a longing I hadn't known was possible and had certainly never felt with any of the boys I'd spent so much time trying to impress at home.

After that first kiss, Taylor and I spent the rest of the summer sneaking every moment alone that we could. We'd spent endless hours making out, touching and exploring each other over our clothes. At sixteen, neither of us had been ready to go all the way with our bodies, but we'd given all of our hearts, professing our love every chance we got.

Ours had been an all-consuming teenage love, the kind of love that made me want to despair at the thought of not being with Taylor, that had me sneaking out of my grandmother's house to meet her for moonlight kisses by the stream and fantasizing about her every moment that we weren't together.

But I'd also been drowning in fear. There was a girl in my class who wore her hair short and dressed in masculine clothes, and I heard the way people made fun of her, the names they called her and the things they said about her behind her back. I wasn't sure I was strong enough to take it. And what if I wasn't gay? Maybe this was just a phase some girls went through.

In the end, I'd panicked as the summer drew to a close. I was terrified of coming out to my parents, certain they'd be horrified and cause a huge scene. Taylor was already out, and I didn't want to disappoint her, so I ran instead. I cut myself off from the girl I loved, burying my heartbreak behind a polished smile as I returned to school. I dated boys—a *lot* of boys—but none of them made me feel anything like what I'd felt with Taylor.

I played it straight all the way through college and lost my virginity to a guy on the tennis team. It had been an underwhelming experience at best. Once I started my career as a financial analyst, working with numbers for a living, I'd finally run a cost-benefit analysis on my own life.

Was it worth it to deny who I was and what I truly wanted just to meet my parents' expectations? By then, it was too late to patch things up with Taylor. We hadn't spoken since we were sixteen. But once I ran the numbers and committed to something, I was all in. So I came out to my parents and started dating women. And I'd finally found peace, the kind of contentment that came from being true to myself and no longer hiding my sexuality or what I wanted.

But something had always been missing. Nothing—not even my relationship with Sabrina—had ever compared to the way it felt when Taylor kissed me, like fireworks were going off inside me, like I could lose myself in that kiss forever, warm and safe and loved. More than that. *Happy.* I'd been so happy that summer.

Now that I was back in Vermont, I was starting to remember just how much I'd left behind here. Not just Taylor, but my grandmother's cabin, the piano, music, dogs, long hikes in the woods, so many things that used to bring me joy.

And maybe it was time to recapture that joy, the way Taylor had done. She was living her life just like she'd always wanted to, doing all the things that made her happy. And she was more beautiful than ever. That ache in my core had only increased during my walk down memory lane, and when I pictured Taylor's face, I felt a throb of arousal so intense that I shoved a hand down the front of my underwear, desperate for release.

I circled my clit, and my hips bucked up to meet my hand, reminding me that I'd neglected myself since I got to Vermont, caught up in my work around the house. My vibrator was still in the duffel bag in the guest room, but right now, I was so turned on, I wasn't even going to need it. I rolled to my belly, thrusting against my fingers as need rose up inside me like a hungry beast, overtaking my senses.

A sharp whine interrupted me, and I wrenched my eyes open to find Violet standing beside the bed, watching me.

I froze. "Shit."

Another whine.

"Violet, go lie down."

The dog yipped, still staring at me. Either she really had to pee, or she was a nosy weirdo. Either way, I couldn't get myself off with her watching. With a groan, I withdrew my hand and sat up, ignoring the unsatisfied ache in my core.

"Fine," I mumbled. "Let's go for a walk."

———

I led the way back into the house five minutes later. As it turned out, Violet had needed to go pretty urgently, so I couldn't really fault her for her inopportune interruption. Once she was squared away, I went down the hall for a shower.

Even though I was alone in the house, I closed the bathroom door behind me, needing a few minutes away from Violet's watchful eyes. It was an adjustment having her around, and honestly, I hoped that once she was settled, she'd give me a little more space. It was unnerving to have her underfoot all the time, quietly staring at me.

Once the water was hot, I stepped into the shower, letting it rush over my face and shoulders, washing away my frustration. A couple of shelter volunteers were coming over this afternoon to give me a crash course in puppy whelping, and then Taylor was stopping by after work to help me put down the laminate flooring. Hopefully it wouldn't be awkward now that I'd apparently started having sex dreams about her.

Where had that come from? I'd gotten over Taylor more than a decade ago. Maybe I was just horny, and my dreams had more to do with that than with Taylor herself. I'd been thinking about her when I fell asleep, so my unconscious mind probably just put two and two together. Surely that was all it was.

My gaze caught on the detachable showerhead. I needed an orgasm or two to get my mind off sex—and Taylor. The ache inside me roared back to life as I lifted the showerhead out of its bracket. It had been a revelation all its own for sixteen-year-old me after a particularly long make-out session with Taylor.

I leaned against the cold wall of the shower as I brought the showerhead between my legs, unsuccessfully stifling a cry as the hot spray met my sensitive skin. I adjusted the angle so the jet of water hit my clit just right, moaning because *God*, that was amazing. My hips moved rhythmically as everything inside me turned hot and tingly.

"Fuck," I cried as release rushed through me, so sharp and powerful, my knees turned to rubber. I slid down the wall to sit in the tub, letting the showerhead coax every last bit of pleasure from my orgasm, and then I let it carry me over the edge a second time, Taylor's name on my lips as endorphins flooded my system, bathing me in pleasure.

I sat slumped against the back of the tub with hot water cascading over my stomach until I'd recovered, and then I got to my feet and finished my shower, feeling like a whole new woman. I dressed and went into the kitchen to fix breakfast for Violet and me. It was weird having a dog that was dependent on me for food and care. I'd never been responsible for anyone's—or anything's—care before.

"Glad you like your new bedding," I said as I mixed up her food. "I don't know about you, but I really needed a good night's sleep."

After we'd both eaten, I took her for a stroll around the yard so she could take care of business, and then I went into the master bedroom to continue packing away my grandma's things. It had been slow going yesterday because I kept getting distracted by memories. I'd spent hours poring over old photo albums before I finally packed those away too.

My summers in Vermont had been some of the happiest times in my childhood, and not just because of Taylor. Back then, my parents fought constantly, often using me as a pawn in their battles. This cabin and my grandma had been a respite from the fighting. My parents finally divorced around the time I started college, and I got along with both of them so much better now that they were happily remarried to new people.

While I worked, Violet lay in her playpen and napped. At least she seemed comfortable in it now. I went into the closet to box up my grandma's shoes for donation, and when I came back out, there was something small and furry in the playpen next to Violet.

"Shit," I blurted. "Oh my God! You had a puppy while I was in the closet?"

I rushed over, trying not to startle her but desperate to see if everything was okay. How had it happened so quickly? As I crouched by the playpen, I saw that there were actually several furry things in there with her, but they weren't puppies. They were stuffed animals from the box of dog toys Taylor had sent over. Violet must have brought them in here to snuggle with.

"Aw, are you nesting?" I asked as my heart turned all warm and mushy. "Is this a thing you do to get ready for motherhood?"

Violet nuzzled one of the stuffed animals and looked at me, quiet and serious as always.

"I think you'll be a good mom." I reached over and rubbed her behind her ears, rewarded by more tail wagging.

Violet's belly twitched, and *oh*, was that a puppy moving? I rubbed my hand down her side, and something moved beneath my fingers.

"That's amazing," I said as I felt it again, a definite wiggle from inside her stomach. It was exciting, but also terrifying because it meant I would soon be looking after puppies.

My phone started to ring where it lay on the bed. I gave Violet one last pat before I stood to get it. My friend Emily was FaceTiming me, and I squealed as I connected the call and her face appeared on my screen. "Em!"

She beamed at me from her couch. "I'm so happy I finally caught you."

"Me too."

"How's Vermont?" she asked. "And tell me about this new foster dog. How did that happen? I want to know everything."

"I see you've been talking to Courtney," I teased as I sat cross-legged in the middle of the bed. I'd FaceTimed with Courtney yesterday, and the three of us generally shared everything. I missed my friends something fierce.

"I have," Emily confirmed. "And from what I gather, there's a girl involved."

"She's just a friend," I said, even though my feelings for Taylor weren't very friendly today. "We knew each other when we were kids."

"And now?" Emily asked.

"Now I barely know her at all," I said, but I knew I was busted by the look on Emily's face. "Fine. We were more than friends when we were teenagers."

"I knew it," Emily said triumphantly. "Oh my God. Was she your first?"

"First kiss, yes, but we never had sex, and it's not why I agreed to the foster dog."

Emily lifted an eyebrow. "Isn't it? Because I don't think you'd bring home a pregnant dog if *I* asked."

I sighed, glancing at Violet, who was asleep in her pen. "Well, maybe I felt like I owed her one because I ran out on her when we were teenagers. But also, the dog is really cute."

"Can I see her?" Emily asked, sounding excited at the prospect. She loved animals, but with two little kids underfoot, she had her hands full at the moment.

"Sure." I slid off the bed and went to sit beside Violet's pen, turning the phone so Emily could see her.

"Aw, she has such a sweet face. I can't wait to see pictures of the puppies," Emily said. "Although I'm glad you're the one dealing with them instead of me. I've got enough butts to wipe as it is."

"Oh God. I don't have to wipe their butts, do I?" I asked, horrified.

Emily shrugged. "I don't know." A shriek echoed from her end of the line, and she made a face. "Sounds like I'd better go check on the munchkins, but call me again soon, okay? I'm going to need frequent Taylor—and puppy—updates."

"Will do, although Taylor's just a friend these days, I swear. Give Noah and Lily a kiss for me."

"You got it." With a wave, Emily disappeared from my screen.

I spent another hour or so packing up my grandma's clothes, and then I went down the hall to wait for Taylor's volunteers Holly and Peyton to arrive. They'd both raised litters of puppies in the past and were going to show me the ropes. While I waited, I sat at the piano and began to play, practicing a few of the songs I would perform at V and V next week.

I heard the click of Violet's nails on the floor and turned to see her walking into the living room. She lay in the dog bed there and watched me play, and I wasn't sure why, but I had the definite impression she liked it. She seemed to relax as she listened, lying with her head between her front paws. Maybe I should play for her more often.

There was a knock at the door, and I stood from the piano. I opened it to find two women standing there. One was a petite blonde with a baby on her hip. The other woman was tall, with dark brown skin and a warm smile.

"Hi," I said, motioning them in. "Thanks so much for coming."

"We're happy to help," the taller woman said. "I'm Holly. It's so nice to meet you."

"And I'm Peyton," the woman with the baby chimed in.

"I'm Phoebe," I told them. "And I'm so glad you're both here. I need all the help I can get."

12

TAYLOR

I arrived at the cabin that evening carrying a box of pizza and a six-pack of my favorite hard cider, ready to spend the evening helping Phoebe put down new floors in the living room. I knocked, and she answered the door wearing purple shorts and a rainbow-striped tank top, her hair piled in its usual messy knot on her head.

"Hi," she said, motioning me in. "Thanks for coming, and dinner is a happy surprise."

"Figured we'd need some fuel," I said as I walked into the kitchen, setting everything down on the table.

Violet got up from her dog bed and walked over, tail wagging.

"She looks more settled today," I said. "How are things?"

"She's nesting, I think," Phoebe told me. "This morning, she brought all the stuffed animals you gave her and put them in her playpen. For a minute, I thought she'd had puppies without me noticing."

"You've been taking her temperature every day?" I asked as I crouched to rub the dog.

Phoebe nodded. "It hasn't dropped yet."

"I think she's close, but I've only witnessed one puppy birth, and Peyton was in charge. I was just watching."

"She and Holly were really helpful when they came over earlier," Phoebe said. "They left me a huge checklist of things to do and watch for."

"I'm glad. Hungry?"

She nodded, and we sat at the table together to eat the pizza while it was hot. I'd gotten a large pie with the works, figuring Phoebe could pick off what she didn't like, but she dove right in, devouring everything from olives to prosciutto.

"This is so good," she mumbled as she wiped her mouth with a napkin and reached for her cider.

"You missed a spot." Without thinking, I leaned over to wipe the sauce from her cheek, but as my thumb met her skin, an electrical charge seemed to jump between us. I drew back, but not before my heart gave a kick in my chest, pulse racing from that simple touch. I really was hopeless where Phoebe was concerned.

She kept eating, but her cheeks were a little bit pinker than they had been a few minutes ago. "Violet likes the new bedding you brought over yesterday."

"Yeah?"

"She slept straight through the night, which was much-needed for both of us."

"I'm glad. I really do think she's settling in well."

"Still, if a more qualified foster home opens up, please let them have her. I'm scared shitless about delivering puppies, and I'm not going to be here long enough to see this through," she said. "I can't afford to stay here two months. I need to go home and get a new job."

I swallowed a mouthful of pizza before answering. "I hear you, and don't worry. I'll figure something out if you leave before the puppies are weaned. Are you job hunting while you're here or waiting until after you get home to start?"

"I'm applying for everything I can find," Phoebe told me. "If I get an in-person interview, I'll just take a day trip down to Boston."

"You work in finance, right?"

She nodded. "I'm a corporate financial analyst. I track a company's financial goals and help them budget and forecast for the future. I was working for a large research firm in Boston before that meme got me fired."

"I can't believe they held that against you," I said, shaking my head. "Like it's your fault someone took a photo of you without your permission and posted it online?"

"Well, I did flip off a guy on a public street, although that doesn't go against anything in the employee handbook—I checked—since I wasn't at work at the time. But after one of our clients recognized me and brought it to their attention, they felt it reflected badly on the company. So, I had to go."

"Still fuckin' sucks," I said.

"It does," she agreed. "I'd been there five years, and I was damn good at my job. I saved them a ton of money over the years."

"I hope their next financial analyst isn't nearly as good," I said, nudging my elbow against hers. "It would serve them right."

She gave me one of those crooked smiles that always made me weak in the knees. "Anyway, I'm still paying for my condo in Boston, and my savings won't last long, so I need a new job, the sooner the better."

I looked down at my half-eaten slice of pizza. "I hope you find one, even better than the one you lost."

"Thanks. Me too."

"Is there anything you could do while you're here?" I asked, shaking off my conflicted feelings about her leaving, because it wasn't her fault she lived in Boston. "Some kind of consulting so you don't burn through all your savings?"

"Hmm, I don't know. I guess I could try, but I don't know who would hire me. I don't have any experience consulting."

"There are a lot of people around here who knew and loved your grandma, though," I said. "And we Vermonters love supporting our own, so if you put up a post on some of the local boards, maybe post a notice in V and V, offering accounting consults or whatever, you might find enough business to tide you over."

"It's definitely something to think about," she said. "Thanks for the idea."

"No problem. Ready to get started on the floors?" I asked.

"Sure. Where are Minnie and Blue tonight?"

"I dropped them off at home before I came over."

"I miss seeing Minnie's happy face," Phoebe said as she polished off her cider and stood from the table. "Sometimes I don't think Violet's happy here."

"Why not?"

One of Phoebe's shoulders lifted. "She doesn't get excited to see me like Minnie does, or you know how dogs seem to smile when their mouths are open and their tongues hang out? Violet doesn't do that either. She just lies around and watches me all day."

"Well, she's still getting settled, and she's probably anxious about giving birth, but she doesn't seem unhappy to me. She looks relaxed, and that's a pretty big deal for a dog in her situation."

"I guess." Phoebe didn't look convinced.

"You're going to have to show me what we're doing here," I said.

She pointed to the boxes of laminate flooring stacked against the wall. "I've already put down the under layer and installed the first row just to get the hang of it. They snap together like big puzzle pieces, so mostly it's just a matter of laying them all down, although we do have to cut the end pieces to fit and stagger them so the pattern looks random, like real hardwood."

"How do you cut them?" I asked.

"With my grandma's circular saw," Phoebe said with a grin. "I've got it set up in back, and while it's slightly terrifying in action, I haven't chopped off any fingers yet."

"I wouldn't have pegged you as a girl who knew how to use a saw, Phoebe Shaw."

"There's a first time for everything."

"All the same, I can cut the rest, if you want," I offered.

"You know how to use a saw?"

"Do I look like I know how to handle a saw?" I asked, because I'd always considered myself a hands-on kind of woman. I knew how to use most kinds of tools and was generally more comfortable working with my hands than with my mouth. My mouth sometimes had a tendency to get me in trouble.

Phoebe's gaze dipped, traversing my plaid cotton top to my khaki shorts before lingering somewhere in the vicinity of my thighs. "I think you can handle a saw," she mumbled, and her cheeks were a perfect match for one of the rosebushes out back.

"Good, because I can." My heart was running a marathon in my chest, and I had no idea what we were even talking about anymore. I could keep myself in check. I'd lusted after Phoebe quietly for years before kissing her, but if she was feeling it too, we might be in trouble, because that was what got us in trouble last time.

Not tonight, though. We got to work, unboxing and laying each piece of laminate flooring. Phoebe let me handle the saw, although she took every opportunity to needle me about it. She'd chosen flooring that was a rich cherry color, and I had to admit, it made the room look a lot bigger and brighter. It would be so much easier to clean too.

Three hours later, it was dark outside, Violet was asleep in her whelping pen in the master bedroom, and I was sweaty and disheveled, but the flooring was finished. The laminate gleamed a bright coppery color beneath the overhead light.

"It's so different," Phoebe said as she sat back on her heels, surveying our work. Her hair got curlier when she sweated, and right now, she had a mass of ringlets around her face that was highly distracting.

"I should go," I said as I rose to my feet. My quads ached from too much time spent crouching over floorboards. "I'll have a mutiny on my hands if I don't get home and feed Minnie soon."

"She *is* dramatic," Phoebe agreed as she stood. "Thanks again for your help tonight."

"It's the least I could do since I'm the one who messed up your renovation plans by giving you a pregnant dog to care for."

"I suppose that's true." She shoved her hands in her front pockets, rocking back on her heels.

I didn't know what to do with my hands either, which meant I needed to go home before I did something I'd regret. "Good night."

"Night."

I let myself out the front door and climbed into my SUV, rolling down the window so I'd get a blast of cool country air as I drove. Hopefully that would clear the romantic nonsense from my head, because I wasn't going there with Phoebe.

Ten minutes later, I pulled into my own driveway. I went down the stairs to my basement apartment to feed and walk the dogs, annoyed every time my thoughts drifted to Phoebe. Once the dogs were settled, I took a shower and went straight to bed, determined to keep a certain brunette out of my dreams.

I was successful too. But when I picked up my phone the next morning, there was a text from Phoebe waiting for me.

Violet's temperature dropped!!!!!!!

13

PHOEBE

My knees hurt. I'd been kneeling on them all afternoon, nailing trim now that the laminate was down. Every half hour or so, I went down the hall to check on Violet. She'd taken to her playpen like a champ now, spending the majority of her time there. She'd evicted the stuffed animals, though, perhaps in anticipation of her real puppies. They were scattered across the floor of the master bedroom.

I scooped them up and dropped them into the toy box as I eyed Violet. Her temperature had dropped this morning, which meant she was likely to go into labor in the next twenty-four hours. "Want to go for a walk?" I asked.

She looked up at me, panting slightly. It was time for her to go outside, but I also hoped the exercise might help get things started. Didn't pregnant women sometimes walk to try to go into labor? I wasn't an expert, but I was pretty sure Emily had done laps at the mall to jumpstart things.

Violet followed me down the hall to the living room. Her toenails made the cutest clicking sound on the laminate floors. I clipped the leash onto her collar and brought her outside. By the time she'd gone down the steps into the yard, she'd stopped panting.

"Wish you could talk," I said. "Then you could tell me if you're in pain. Don't be stoic about it, okay? I need to know you're in labor in time to get someone out here to help us."

She whined when she squatted to pee, which was unusual. Then we walked around the yard together, and I couldn't be sure, but I thought she looked uncomfortable. And since I did *not* want to do this on my own, I was going to call in the reinforcements early and hope it didn't turn out to be a false alarm. I dialed Taylor's number.

"Hi," she answered. "Is it puppy time?"

"I'm not sure, but I think so, and I just…I'd feel so much better if somebody came out and checked her for me."

"Let me make a few calls. I'll have someone at your house within the hour, okay?"

"Thank you," I said, immensely relieved to know that someone knowledgeable would be here soon to help me. I ended the call and took Violet back inside.

She went down the hall to lie in her playpen. She'd seemed to like it when I played the piano yesterday, so I sat on the bench and began to play, hoping it would soothe her. I wasn't paying attention to a specific song or melody, just letting my fingers roam the keyboard. It was a method my grandmother had taught me before I'd started taking formal lessons.

But after a few minutes, I realized I wasn't playing a random tune at all. The familiar notes of Alicia Keys's "No One" filled the living room. It had been our song, mine and Taylor's. I would sit right here at this piano and play it for her, not that my voice held a candle to Alicia's. My fingers kept moving, and I began to sing along, quietly at first and picking up volume as I got lost in the music.

It was as familiar as it was emotional, memories of that summer flowing through me as the lyrics spilled from my mouth. We'd been so much in love. As I sang our song, I remembered the way I used to lie beside Taylor, hands entwined, staring into each other's eyes as we talked for hours, the way my body seemed to inflate with happiness when she came into a room, the way it felt when she wrapped her arms around me and kissed me until my whole body thrummed with electricity.

There was a knock at the door, and I stopped playing, wrenched from my romantic trance back to the real world where there was a dog down the hall who was about to have puppies and someone from the shelter at my door to help me through it. I stood and walked to the door, and my heart lurched against my ribs when I saw Taylor on the front porch.

Her hair was in a ponytail, and she was wearing a T-shirt with the shelter's logo on it as if she'd come straight from work. She looked slightly dazed, as if she'd heard what song I was playing. With the windows wide open to let in the spring air, she probably had. I gulped, my throat gone dry.

"Hi," she said, her hazel eyes locked on mine with a dizzying intensity.

Maybe I was still stuck in the past, but that fluttery feeling in my belly was exactly the way it had felt when she looked at me that summer. *Oof.* "Hi."

"How's Violet?" she asked as she walked past me into the house.

"Um, she's in her playpen. I was just playing some music for her. She seems to like it when I play the piano."

"That was good thinking," Taylor said. "If the piano calms her, you should keep playing."

"Unless it bothers you."

She glanced over her shoulder at me, already heading toward the master bedroom. "You know it doesn't."

I followed her down the hall to find Violet in her playpen, panting heavily. She stood as Taylor approached, and that's when I noticed she was shaking. Oh boy. This was really happening.

"Looks like you were right," Taylor said, crouching in front of Violet. "Shaking and panting are both early signs of labor."

"Yeah," I agreed. This was exactly what Holly and Peyton had told me to watch for. "I wasn't expecting to see you tonight, though."

"Peyton's daughter is running a fever, and Holly's working tonight, so you're stuck with me."

"Well, I'm not complaining." Shit. Did that sound flirty? I hadn't meant for it to.

Taylor stood, giving me an amused look. "I'm not either. It'll be fun to watch some new lives enter the world."

"What do we do now?"

"Just keep an eye on her, mostly," Taylor said. "She knows what to do. You could see if she wants to go outside before her labor progresses, in case she needs to pee or anything."

"Oh yeah, okay." I looked at Violet. "Want to go outside?"

She got right out of her playpen and headed down the hall. Taylor and I followed. I put Violet on leash, and we all went into the backyard. Violet took care of business, whining as she squatted, and I hoped she wasn't about to deliver a puppy right there in the yard, because she definitely looked uncomfortable.

But she headed for the back door, and when I opened it for her, she went inside for a drink of water and then straight down the hall to her playpen.

"We should get our supplies ready," Taylor said. "She may or may not need any help, but it's best to be prepared."

I went to the box in the corner that Taylor had brought on Monday. It contained old towels, a bulb syringe, scissors, iodine, absorbent pads, and probably a few other things I couldn't see from the top. With Taylor's guidance, we placed pads in Violet's playpen to help contain any messes, sterilized the scissors, and set everything out for easy access.

Violet moved around restlessly in the pen, nipping at the bedding as she tried to get it just right now that we'd added the pads. Then she plopped down in the middle and lay, panting.

"There's really not much else we can do but wait," Taylor said. "It could still be a few hours, so we should probably give her some space and just keep checking in."

"Did you come straight from work?" I asked.

Taylor nodded. "I asked Alleya, who I work with, to take Minnie and Blue home with her tonight, in case I'm here awhile."

"Oh." The thought of Taylor being here awhile was both thrilling and unnerving, because it meant we'd be here alone, late at night, potentially sitting together on my grandmother's bed. "Want me to fix us something to eat while we wait?"

"Sure. I'm pretty hungry, actually."

"Should I feed Violet her supper?" I asked as I went down the hall to the kitchen.

"It's better if you wait and feed her after she's delivered the puppies. She's probably not even hungry right now. We'll make sure to offer her lots of water, though."

"Makes sense," I said. "I was going to roast a chicken, if that sounds good to you."

"A whole chicken just for you?" Taylor asked as she poured herself a glass of water. Her familiarity with the kitchen cabinets was another reminder of how much time she'd spend here with my grandma over the years. More than I had, apparently.

"I like the leftovers for sandwiches, and well…I thought Violet might want some, but shhhh, don't tell that lady from the shelter that I feed her people food, okay?"

Taylor grinned. "I knew you were a softie deep down."

"Nope. Nothing but barbed wire in here." I jabbed a finger against my ribs before opening the fridge. I took out the chicken and seasoned it with herbs and lemon juice. Then I chopped some carrots and potatoes and put it all in the oven. "Want some pretzel sticks while it cooks?"

"You've always been a fan of pretzel sticks," Taylor said. "Sure."

I got out the bag of pretzels and poured some into a bowl, and then I grabbed two Shipley ciders from the fridge. They were left over from the six-pack Taylor had brought yesterday when we put down the laminate flooring. I wasn't always a fan of hard cider, but this was good, and it was local too.

We each popped open a bottle, and Taylor went to check on Violet. I turned on the TV to save us from having to come up with enough conversation to fill the evening. My dad had canceled the cable months ago, so I logged into my Netflix account and put on a nature documentary. Taylor did love nature, after all.

"Nothing yet," she said as she came back into the living room. She sat beside me on the couch, and we ate pretzels and drank cider while we watched a band of monkeys in Malaysia battle over territory. Every ten minutes or so, Taylor went to check on Violet.

I was just getting invested in the outcome of the territory war when Taylor called from the bedroom.

"I think it's time," she said.

"Oh shit." I bolted off the couch, almost knocking over my cider in my hurry. When I got to the bedroom, Violet was in the middle of her playpen, and even my untrained eyes could see she was pushing.

"You're doing great, Violet," Taylor said in a quiet, soothing voice. "What a good girl. You're going to be such a good mama."

I sat beside her on the bed, heart pounding as we watched Violet. We took turns encouraging her, because she was *really* pushing now, and her eyes looked kind of wild and frantic. I didn't want to get in her way since we hadn't known each other that long, but she kept looking at me when I spoke to her, and occasionally, her tail gave what might have been a small wag, which made me think she didn't mind us being here with her.

"Oh," I whispered. "Is that…is that a puppy?"

Something was starting to protrude beneath her tail. Violet turned around to sniff at it, giving it a few hesitant licks.

"It sure is," Taylor said, sounding as awed as I felt.

"I've never watched anything be born before." I pressed a hand against my chest, where my heart was still beating frantically, overwhelmed by the moment.

Violet gave another big push, and the puppy slid the rest of the way out. It looked black or maybe dark brown, still inside its birth sack. I gasped, and my hand slid into Taylor's. She gave it a tight squeeze.

"What do we do?" I whispered.

"Nothing yet. Let's give her a chance to take care of it on her own," Taylor said quietly. "She needs to bite through the membrane and lick its face to clear the airways."

We watched, transfixed, as Violet sniffed the puppy. Just when I was starting to get nervous, she nipped at the membrane, licking and biting until she revealed a perfect chocolate-brown puppy with one white paw. She kept licking, rocking its little body back and forth with her tongue, and it mewled, tiny paws waving in the air.

"Oh wow." My eyes were unexpectedly moist. "She did it."

"She sure did," Taylor said. "Great job, Violet. What a beautiful baby you made."

"It's so little." I'd never seen a newborn puppy before. This one was still wet, and its eyes were closed, ears flat against its head, giving it an odd, almost seal-like appearance.

"Can I have a quick look?" Taylor asked gently, lowering herself to the floor. She scooted closer to Violet, moving slowly so she didn't startle the dog.

Violet watched closely but didn't object when Taylor touched the puppy and then picked it up. She rubbed it with a cloth, helping to dry it, talking reassuringly to Violet the whole time. Then she peeked under the puppy's tail before settling it against Violet's belly.

She turned to me with a triumphant smile. "It's a girl!"

TAYLOR

Violet licked and nuzzled her puppy as it began to nurse. Since everything seemed to be going well, I returned to the bed, sitting beside Phoebe. "I want to get her used to us handling them, and I also need to make sure their airways are clear and nothing's visibly amiss, but it seems like Violet's going to do the rest of the work for us. She's doing a great job so far."

"The puppy is so little," Phoebe said, glossy-eyed with a big, giddy smile on her face.

Her joy over watching the puppy's birth was going to be my undoing, because nothing made me softer than a woman who loved rescue dogs. "Do you want to name her?" I asked.

Phoebe's head bobbed. "Oh please, can I?"

"You can name the whole litter if you want."

Her expression turned thoughtful. "Okay. I'm going to have to give this some thought. You said there are four, right?"

"The vet saw four on the X-ray, but it's possible a fifth puppy was hiding," I told her.

"Four's a good number," Phoebe said. "It's the smallest squared prime."

"I have no idea what that means." I nudged my shoulder against hers. I'd never understood her when she started talking about math, but once upon a time, her math geekiness had been a huge turn-on for me.

"Two squared," Phoebe said. "Two is the smallest prime number."

"You're going to give them math names, aren't you?"

She narrowed her eyes at me. "I can name them anything I want. You said so."

I could feel my lips stretching into a smile. "But remember, cute names will appeal to adopters, although honestly, puppies are usually pretty easy to find homes for. These are pitties or pit mixes, though, and there are a lot of people who're hesitant about the breed for the same reasons you were."

Phoebe shook her head. "I've changed my mind about them. I can't imagine Violet biting anyone."

"Well, she might if she felt threatened. A lot of dogs will bite if you push them far enough, but she's no more likely to bite than any other dog."

"There's something so pure about her," Phoebe said, her tone hushed. "She just wants a quiet, comfortable life. She doesn't have an agenda beyond the basic creature comforts."

"That's the beauty of animals," I told her. "They don't have agendas."

"I like that," she said.

"Maybe once you're back in Boston, you should get a pet," I suggested.

"Well, my condo doesn't allow them, but I could get a fish or something."

"Fun fact: there are fish rescues," I told her. "Adopt, don't shop."

"Fish rescues?" she asked incredulously.

"Yep. You can rescue pretty much any kind of pet you might want."

"Cool. Oh!" Phoebe sat up straight, staring toward the whelping box. "I think she's pushing again."

I followed her gaze. Violet, who had been quietly licking her first puppy while she nursed, had tensed up. "You're right."

Phoebe slid her hand into mine, the way she'd done when the first puppy was born, and I couldn't resist squeezing it. Hand in hand, we watched as another puppy was born. This one was mostly white, with several brown patches. Once Violet cleaned it up, I gave it a quick check.

"Boy," I told Phoebe.

She beamed at the news. "One of each." A beep echoed from the kitchen, and her eyes widened. "I forgot all about the chicken."

"So did I, but I'm starving. Shall we leave her to nurse these two for a few minutes and go eat?"

"Will she be okay?" Phoebe asked, adorably concerned about the dog she hadn't wanted to bring home.

I nodded. "There's usually a gap of about thirty minutes between puppies, and we'll just be in the kitchen. We'll keep checking on her."

"'Kay," Phoebe said, sliding to her feet. She pushed down her shorts, which had ridden up to reveal that little brown birthmark I used to trace with my fingers.

I followed her to the kitchen, and together, we carved the chicken and fixed two plates. We popped open fresh ciders and sat at the kitchen table to eat.

"Should I bring her some chicken?" she asked.

I shook my head. "She's content with her puppies right now. With any luck, she'll be finished in an hour or so, and you can spoil her with chicken then. In fact, you should spoil her all you want until they're weaned. She'll need lots of calories. Just don't feed her from the table. We don't want to give her any bad habits for her next owner."

"Right." Phoebe nodded. "I'll spoil her politely."

I took a bite of my chicken. It was juicy and flavorful. I loved the combination of the tangy lemon juice with the other seasonings she'd added. "This is good."

"Thanks. It's one of my staples because it's easy and it feeds me for multiple meals."

"Yeah, I like those too," I said. "I freeze my leftovers so I can pull out an easy meal later in the week when I need it."

"Cooking for one is a pain," she agreed, and something wistful passed over her expression, reminding me that she'd been in a serious relationship until very recently. Or at least, I assumed it had been serious.

"Do you miss her?" I asked. "Your ex-girlfriend? And please tell me to butt out if that's too personal."

Her lips twisted to the side. "I do, and I don't, if that makes sense."

"I think it does." Actually, it was sort of how I'd felt after Phoebe left me.

"I miss her," Phoebe said quietly, "but I'm not sure I could ever forgive her, so hopefully the part of me that's missing her gets over it soon."

"It will," I told her.

Phoebe gave me a sharp look, as if she'd just realized what experience I was drawing from with my words. "We should get back to Violet."

"Yes," I agreed, rushing through the last few bites of my meal. We put our dishes in the sink and brought our cider with us back to the master bedroom.

Violet was right where we'd left her, nursing her first two puppies. Phoebe and I sat on the bed, drinking cider and talking quietly while we waited for the next puppy to arrive. It didn't take long. Violet delivered a fawn-colored puppy with a white blaze on its face much like her own. The puppy was her mirror image except that it was a boy.

I cleared away the afterbirth and set the puppy against her with the other two to nurse while Phoebe brought Violet's water bowl into the bedroom to offer her a drink.

"She's such a trooper," Phoebe said as she held the bowl out to Violet. "It's amazing how animals just know what to do."

"It really is," I agreed. "Instincts are fascinating to me."

"One more to go," Phoebe said as she rejoined me on the bed.

"Or maybe two if Violet decides to keep us on our toes."

"Right." Phoebe twirled one of her curls around her index finger, and I had to look away to keep from remembering how I used to do that. I loved playing with her hair. "I have to admit, this is less stressful than I was anticipating," she said. "I was pretty freaked out about the whole thing, but now I feel like I can relax and enjoy watching the last puppy be born."

"I'm glad," I told her. "Hopefully, the next few weeks will be less stressful than you're anticipating too."

"What will I need to do with them?" she asked.

"Not too much, as long as Violet's taking care of them, and things are off to a good start on that front. You'll need to weigh each puppy every day to make sure they're gaining weight. That's generally more of a concern in a bigger litter, in case someone is getting pushed aside and not getting enough milk. But the first sign of a lot of health problems in puppies is a failure to gain weight."

"Oh geez," Phoebe said. "I wasn't worried about health problems, but now I am."

I laughed. "You probably don't have anything to worry about, and if you have any concerns at all, just call me. I'll have you bring them in for a couple of vet checks and their first vaccinations, and we'll talk about weaning later. For the first week or so, all you really have to do is weigh them and make sure they look healthy."

"All right, but you should probably still be prepared for me to call with a million questions," she said, watching Violet and the puppies.

"Any time."

"What do you think the fourth puppy will be?" she asked, turning those warm brown eyes on me. "Boy or girl? And what color?"

"Are we taking bets or what?"

"Sure. Loser buys dinner next Friday before my set at V and V." She paused, frowning. "Wait. Can I leave her like that?"

"I can ask Holly or Peyton to come and check on her for you if you like," I told her, "so you can still perform at V and V."

"And dinner?" she asked.

I hesitated. That felt a bit like a date, and I didn't want to go there, but Phoebe was trying really hard to be friendly, and she'd done an awfully big favor for me. "Sure."

"Cool. So, the winner picks the restaurant, and the loser pays. I'm betting she'll even things out with another girl, mostly white with some brown spots."

"I'll say boy, then. Solid black."

"Black?" Phoebe's eyebrows raised. "But Violet's not black, and neither are any of the other puppies."

I shrugged. "I have a thing for black dogs, but if it's brown, I guess we'll have to decide whether it's closer to my guess or yours."

"A judgment call," Phoebe agreed. "All right, Violet. Now it's on you. One more puppy—hopefully—and you'll be done."

I took a swig of cider, watching Violet. The puppies had tired themselves out and gone to sleep, and she was panting and starting to look restless, like another one was on the way. Sure enough, not five minutes later, she started to push. A white nose began to emerge, and Phoebe let out a little squeal beside me.

"I think you're going to be buying me dinner next Friday," she whispered.

"Let's not get ahead of ourselves," I said, but the truth was, I wouldn't mind buying her dinner. Maybe we deserved a nice night out to put away any residual hurt from the past and move on. It really wasn't fair of me to hold the things she'd done in high school against her. She'd been young and scared, and teenagers had never been known for their excellent decision-making skills, after all.

Still, she was only in town for a few weeks, which meant I

needed to keep her in the friend zone. I wasn't going to get my heart broken by the same woman twice.

"Here it comes," Phoebe whispered as Violet gave another big push.

The puppy slid out, landing on the clean pad I'd put there. This one was a dark color with a white face, although it was hard to tell yet whether it was brown or black. It also appeared to be smaller than the other three. Violet immediately got busy removing the sack and cleaning it up. She seemed to be an old pro by now.

"It might come down to the gender to decide the winner," Phoebe said in a hushed voice.

"Mm," I agreed, but there was an unsettled feeling in my gut. The puppy hadn't cried yet, and I couldn't tell if it was moving. As I watched, Violet pushed it away with her nose, turning back to her other puppies.

I shoved my cider into Phoebe's hand and slid off the bed, grabbing a towel as I hurried to the whelping box. I took the small, limp puppy in one hand, rubbing its chest vigorously with the towel.

"Is something wrong?" Phoebe asked.

I looked down at the motionless puppy in my hands. "It's not breathing."

15

PHOEBE

"Oh no," I gasped, watching as Taylor rubbed the puppy's chest while it lay motionless in her hands. I'd been so caught up in betting over its gender and appearance, I'd gotten cocky. I'd assumed we were out of the woods, and now the puppy might die.

"Come on, little one," Taylor said. She cleared the puppy's airway and blew gently into its mouth before returning to rubbing its chest with the towel. Her movements were brisk, almost rough, and the puppy's little body flopped limply from side to side.

There was a sick feeling in the pit of my stomach, and my heart was beating too fast. I desperately wanted to look away because I didn't want to see this, but I couldn't seem to take my eyes off that tiny lifeless puppy.

"Please, please, please…" I chanted. I put our ciders on the nightstand and clasped my hands in front of me. It felt like it had been ages since the puppy was born, but probably only a minute or two had passed. Still, I'd taken countless breaths in the meantime while the puppy hadn't taken a single one. As much as I wanted Taylor to keep going, as much as I wanted a miracle to happen, it seemed like it had been too long.

The puppy was dead.

I groaned, squeezing my eyes shut. What an awful end to what had been such a wonderful experience. A tiny, high-pitched squeak startled me, and my eyes popped open to see the puppy twitch in Taylor's hands. It squeaked again as its paws began to flail.

"Holy shit," I breathed. "You really did it. You brought that puppy back to life."

"I did," Taylor said, sounding awestruck.

Violet began to sniff the new puppy, perhaps drawn by its cries. Taylor gave it another rub and then set it against Violet's belly to nurse. I slid off the bed to sit beside Taylor, watching as the new puppy latched on for its first drink of milk.

"It's a girl," Taylor said.

"And she's almost solid black." I took Taylor's hand as tears glazed my vision.

"Guess we might need a tie breaker for our bet."

"I can't believe you saved her." I swiped at my eyes with my free hand, and Taylor turned toward me.

"Sometimes, they just need a little kickstart," she said.

"I wouldn't have been able to do that for her. You saved her life." I wrapped my arms around her in an impulsive hug.

Taylor's arms came around me, hugging me back. Her heart thumped against my right breast, as fast and frantic as my own. She'd been scared too. My cheek was pressed against hers, and when I started to pull away, her arms tightened, drawing me back in, but this time, my mouth met hers. I sucked in a startled breath. Taylor did too.

Her eyes widened, honeyed brown swimming with flecks of green and gold. I used to tell her that she had the whole universe in her eyes. They were so beautiful, maybe the most beautiful thing about her, but it was a toss-up, because I had loved every inch of her.

I hadn't meant to kiss her, but now that I had, I wanted more. My tongue traced the seam of her lips, and she moaned, parting them for me. I deepened the kiss, tasting apple cider in the hot depths of her mouth. Her fingers grasped the fabric of my top, yanking me closer. Our breasts collided, and a warm tingle spread through my belly.

I cupped her face in my hands, and the familiar contour of her cheekbones beneath my fingertips felt like a homecoming. And then, just as quickly as it had started, she pushed me away. I sat back on my heels, staring at her in surprise. Taylor's cheeks were rosy, and she pressed one hand against her mouth.

"I'm sorry," she murmured.

"No," I said, breathing hard. "It's okay. That was… We shouldn't…"

"No, we shouldn't," she repeated firmly. "And not just because we should be watching Violet and her puppies right now."

"You're right." I swallowed, disappointment squelching the fire in my belly.

"I can't do this with you." A muscle in her jaw flexed. She turned away, facing Violet and the puppies. "It's a terrible idea for a lot of reasons."

"I know."

"You aren't staying," she said quietly.

"Right." Which meant if we *did* start anything, I'd have to leave her all over again. She was right. That was a terrible idea.

"The puppy's nursing well," she said, refocusing the conversation as if our kiss had never happened.

"Do you think she'll be okay?"

"Probably," she said. "The cord might have gotten compressed while she was being born, in which case, she's out of danger, but we'll keep an eye on her just in case it's something more serious. She's smaller than the others."

I wrapped my arms around myself, chilled by the absence of Taylor's embrace. "How will I know? I'm going to worry about her all night."

"I'll stay until everyone's settled," Taylor said, but the look she gave me was wary. She hadn't forgotten about our kiss any more than I had.

We moved to sit on the bed again, giving Violet some room now that the newest puppy was out of immediate danger. The dynamic between us was different now, though. Taylor left several feet of space between us, and she wasn't looking at me. An awkward silence enveloped the bedroom.

I hugged my knees against my chest, watching as Violet licked and nuzzled her puppies. Hopefully, she was finished, and there were only four. The littlest one's dramatic arrival hadn't made me any more confident about fostering them. In fact, I was terrified, but I wasn't about to cause any extra tension between me and Taylor by voicing my concerns out loud.

The newest puppy seemed to be nursing well, but every time I looked at her, I just saw her limp body in Taylor's hand. It sent a shiver over my skin. I reached for my cider and polished it off. After a few minutes, the puppies had all fallen asleep, and Violet looked pretty relaxed too, head down and eyes closed.

Taylor stood. "I think she's finished, so I'm going to get her cleaned up."

"Okay."

Taylor created a little nest out of clean towels on the floor and carefully placed the sleeping puppies inside it. They mewled and squirmed, crawling against each other for warmth. Violet stood, walking over to check them. "They're fine, sweet girl," Taylor told her. "Let me just get you and your bed cleaned up, and you can have them right back. Phoebe, can you wet this towel for me? I need it warm, but not hot." She held a towel in my direction.

I slid off the bed and took the towel from her. I went into the master bathroom and ran my fingers under the water until it was comfortably warm. Then I wet the towel and brought it back to Taylor. She'd already stripped all the bedding out of the playpen. The absorbent pads she'd refreshed throughout Violet's labor had caught most of the mess, but even so, the bedding needed a wash.

I handed the towel to Taylor and picked up the blanket and

towels, carrying them down the hall to the washing machine. Hopefully, Violet wouldn't mind if her new bedding didn't smell like her former owner. When I returned to the bedroom, Taylor had finished cleaning Violet and was putting fresh bedding in the playpen.

"Violet, do you want to go outside?" I asked. "Outside?" I repeated, since that seemed to be the word she recognized.

She gave me a quick tail wag before following me down the hall. I clipped on her leash and brought her out back. She whined as she peed, and I winced in sympathy. She had to be sore, but she seemed to be doing well, all things considered. Animals were so resilient.

"Want supper?" I asked when we were back inside, picking up her food bowl for emphasis.

She wagged her tail, watching expectantly.

"Only give her a small meal," Taylor called from the bedroom. "You can give her another small meal in a few hours or when you wake up in the morning."

"Got it." I mixed together her dry kibble with some canned puppy food and then put a few pieces of roasted chicken on top. When I set the bowl on the floor, Violet dug in enthusiastically.

She ate her dinner and had a big drink of water before going down the hall to check on her babies. Taylor got her settled in the playpen with them, and Violet licked them while they squirmed and squealed as they crawled over each other to find a spot to nurse.

"You'll need to bring them all in to see the vet tomorrow," Taylor told me. "They just need a quick checkup to make sure everyone's doing well."

"At the shelter?" I asked.

"We don't have a full-time vet, but we have one we work with. She should be able to fit you in if you give her a call first thing."

I nodded. "Okay."

"Just tell her you're fostering for us. She's got our payment information on file, so it won't cost you anything. I'll text you her info."

"Are you leaving?" I squeezed my hands together, glancing at the clock. It was almost midnight. Wow. The whole evening had gone by without me realizing it.

"I don't think there's anything else I can do here tonight," she told me. "You just need to watch Violet for any sign of complications." Taylor rattled off a long list of things that would require an emergency call to the vet, each one sounding more alarming than the last. "And you should keep taking her temperature daily. If she spikes a fever, it could indicate that she has an infection."

"Do you have a checklist you can send me?" I asked, because this felt overwhelming, and my brain was whirling trying to keep track. I liked numbers and lists, items I could check off once I'd completed them.

Taylor nodded. "I've got several resources and links I can send you."

"Thank you."

"And feel free to call me anytime with questions." She stood and headed toward the living room.

I followed, my stomach squirming with discomfort. I wasn't ready to be left alone with the puppies. What if something went wrong? What if the little one stopped breathing again? What if a surprise fifth puppy arrived? And I really felt like we should address that kiss before she left, but I had no idea what to say, and clearly Taylor didn't want to talk about it.

With a wave, she grabbed her bag and went out the front door.

I walked down the hall to check on Violet. She was stretched out flat on her side, fast asleep with the puppies snuggled against her belly. Well, at least they were relaxed. I only wished I could say the same. I changed into my pajamas and went into the bathroom to wash up for bed. I should at least try to get some sleep, although I was sure I was going to be up all night watching and worrying over the puppies.

I had just climbed into bed when I heard tires crunching over gravel and saw the sweep of headlights through the window. Who was at my house at this time of night? If this were anywhere but Vermont, I might have been worried. The car door opened, and a woman got out. A shaft of light from my bedroom window washed over her face.

It was Taylor.

TAYLOR

The front door opened to reveal Phoebe silhouetted in the door-way, giving me a puzzled look. She wore striped sleep shorts and a thin tank top, her hair loose over her shoulders, and my brain short-circuited at the sight.

"Taylor? What are you doing back here?" she asked as she beckoned me inside.

"I, um, I forgot my phone." I stepped past her, trying not to notice the way her nipples poked against the fabric of her tank top or the damp glow on her face, suggesting she'd just washed it.

"Oh, okay."

"Sorry to barge in on you while you were getting ready for bed." I glanced around the kitchen and living room, trying to remember where I'd left my phone.

"Totally fine," she said. "I'm honestly a little freaked out to be alone tonight anyway."

"What?" I turned to look at her.

Phoebe's bottom lip was pinched between her teeth. "I keep staring at the little one, trying to make sure she's still breathing. What if I fall asleep, and when I wake up, she's dead?"

"Then she probably would have died anyway, whether you were asleep or not," I told her. "But I think she's fine. I really do."

"I hope so. Your phone's probably in the bedroom."

"Right." I walked down the hall. Violet looked up at me from her spot in the whelping box, and her tail thumped against the bedding. She was curled around the puppies, looking like a proud mama. She seemed to have settled into motherhood like a champ. And there was my phone, lying facedown on the floor beside her.

I stooped to pick it up, and then I reached for the smallest puppy, moving slowly and making sure I had Violet's permission to touch her. But the dog remained relaxed, watching as I lifted her baby. "I'll just give her another check before I leave, okay?" I said to Phoebe, hoping that would ease her mind, because there was no way I was staying the night, not after that kiss.

"Thank you," she said, crouching beside me. "You know, we never decided who won the bet."

"No, we didn't." I held the puppy on my palms, watching her breathe, but I didn't see any signs of distress. Her nose and mouth were a nice healthy pink, and she whimpered, rolling over in my hands, paws flailing.

"Now that she's dry, she's actually brown, not black," Phoebe said, leaning over my shoulder to look at the puppy, which put her way too close to me. The puppy was indeed a dark chocolate brown, with a white face.

I didn't turn my head to look at Phoebe. "And you predicted a brown-and-white female puppy, so I'd say you won."

"I guess that means you're buying dinner next Friday." She reached over to rub the puppy before I set her back in the box with Violet.

I stood, facing her. "I don't know if dinner's such a good idea."

"Sure it is," Phoebe said. "I'd really like to spend some time with you that doesn't involve puppies, Taylor."

I hesitated, hands shoved into the pockets of my jeans.

"Just as friends," Phoebe insisted. "I want to be friends, don't you?"

Well, when she put it that way… "Fine, I guess."

She rolled her eyes at me. "Don't sound so enthusiastic."

"I'm tired," I deflected. "But yes, dinner next Friday. In the meantime, try to get some sleep. I'll call you in the morning to check in and see how everyone's doing."

She nodded. "Thanks."

"Good night, Phoebe," I said. Then I headed for the door before I lost all my common sense and succumbed to her unasked request for me to stay.

The next day, I stopped by Phoebe's cabin on my lunch break, leaving Minnie and Blue in my office. I'd talked to Phoebe briefly that morning to confirm that everyone was doing okay. She sounded tired but didn't have anything alarming to report. The puppies were all nursing well and gaining weight.

I walked up the steps to the front door and knocked. She pulled it open wearing a sunny yellow dress. It was a simple cotton T-shirt dress, but on Phoebe, it looked like a million bucks, emphasizing her tanned legs and the golden highlights in her hair. Yellow was definitely her color.

"How's everyone doing?" I asked as she invited me inside.

"Good, I think." She gave me a sheepish smile. "I guess I can stop watching the little one breathe. The vet said she looked fine."

"That's great news," I said. "Have you thought about names yet?"

She shook her head. "I'm too tired today to come up with anything cute."

"Well, let me know when you decide. I'll put pictures of them on our blog, so that our supporters can follow along on their journey. That'll help generate interest for when we're ready to start accepting adoption applications for them."

"I've already taken *lots* of pictures," she told me. "I'll send you some for the blog."

"Perfect." I followed her down the hall, where Violet and the puppies were in their whelping box. Violet's tail began to wag when she saw me. "She's settled in so well here with you."

"Well, I really haven't done much," Phoebe said. "But I'm glad she doesn't hate me."

"Sorry for complicating your time in Vermont."

"I'm not as annoyed about it as I thought I would be." And her smile didn't look annoyed at all. "I just don't know what will happen to them when I go back to Boston. I don't like feeling like I'm responsible for uprooting their lives."

"You aren't," I told her. "Sometimes dogs have to switch foster homes. It happens a lot, actually. It isn't ideal, but like I told you before, we do the best we can. It's still better for them than being in the shelter."

I sat in front of Violet's pen to look at the puppies while Phoebe flopped on the bed. The pups were all sleeping at the moment, so I spent a few minutes rubbing Violet. I didn't want her to feel left out now that her little ones had arrived.

"You know," I said to Phoebe. "If you don't want to uproot their lives, you could just sell me the house, and I'll move in with Minnie and Blue, and they can all stay here until they find homes." I was just teasing—mostly—but I also wasn't going to give up on buying this house until the rental lockbox was on the front door and Phoebe had left town.

"Taylor…"

"Did you even tell your dad I'm interested in buying?" I asked.

"No," she said.

"Will you? Please?"

"He's not going to change his mind," she said, and I couldn't tell if her tone was annoyed or just resigned.

"You said he wants to keep the house in the family, but maybe that was when he thought he'd be selling to a total stranger. Your family has known mine for decades, and if I move in here, I'm not moving out. Burlington is my home, and this house is right up the street from my parents. I'd fill it with rescue dogs and live here happily ever after."

"What about a family of your own?" she asked quietly.

"Sure," I said. "I'd love one if I meet the right woman."

"Tell me about her," Phoebe said, watching me from the bed. "What do you think she'll be like?"

I shrugged, because the image that immediately filled my brain was a petite pain in my ass with curly brown hair and eyes like melted chocolate. "Well, she'd have to be an animal lover."

"Of course," Phoebe agreed.

"And she'd have to love the outdoors and be happy with a simple life here in Vermont. No big-city dreams."

"No?" she asked, watching me closely out of those chocolate eyes.

"Nope. I love it here, and I never want to leave. Vermont is in my blood."

"Vacations?" Phoebe asked.

"I haven't taken many of those," I said thoughtfully. "But I'm not opposed to the idea. I might like to travel if I had someone to do it with and someone to watch my dogs."

"I'm sure dog sitters exist around here," she said, looking amused.

"I'm certain you're right," I agreed.

"Then all you need is the right woman to share your life with."

"Hmm." I stroked the brown-and-white-spotted puppy, who had woken and was nuzzling against Violet, looking for his next meal. "Well, I'm here ready and waiting."

But in that moment, it was hard to imagine a woman more perfect than Phoebe, except for the fact that she didn't live in Vermont.

PHOEBE

I pressed my nose against a bright red rose and inhaled, intoxicated by its sweet fragrance. Violet stood beside me, nose up and sniffing as if she was enjoying my grandmother's rosebushes too. I figured she might want a little break from being crawled over and sucked on, so we were taking a stroll around the backyard together.

Now that I'd gotten to know her a little better, I could tell when she was relaxed. Her tail went up, and she would sniff around like she was interested in her surroundings instead of just watching me like I might do something traitorous if she let her guard down. And right now, she looked awfully content. Maybe motherhood had mellowed her.

"We need to name your puppies," I told her.

She looked up at me and wagged her tail. It had only been three days since they were born, but I was already tired of having to describe them when Taylor called for updates. "The brown one with the white blaze gained two ounces today."

They needed names. And as I leaned in to smell another rose, I had a flash of inspiration. What if I named them after types of roses? That would be cute, and it was meaningful to my grandma.

"Let's get you back inside and google some roses," I said to Violet.

We went in through the back door, and she got a big drink of water. It wasn't time for her next meal yet, but I gave her a couple of dog biscuits because she was a nursing mama and she deserved snacks, as far as I was concerned.

After Violet finished crunching through her biscuits, she went down the hall like a dutiful mom, curling up in her pen to let the puppies nurse. I sat on the bed and searched types of roses on my phone. The first one that caught my eye was Blaze. That was a perfect name for the brown male puppy with the white blaze on his face.

"One down, three to go," I said, scrolling through more photos of roses. "Oh, there's one called Queen Elizabeth." I looked at the brown female puppy with her one white paw, the first puppy born. She also had the loudest cry and used it often. "The monarch is always the firstborn, and you're kind of a drama queen. We can just call you Elizabeth for short."

Next, I eyed the white puppy with brown spots. "What about Sunsprite? We could call you Sunny. That's masculine enough, right?"

Violet watched me, sprawled on her side while they nursed. That only left the littlest puppy, the one that had given us such a scare. She was a rich chocolate brown with a white face.

"I've got it," I told her. "Cherry Parfait, and we'll call you Cherry, because you're little. What do you think, Violet? Do you like the names I picked?"

She thumped her tail against the dog bed.

"I'll take that as a yes. Okay, I'm going to take pictures of each puppy and text them to Taylor with their new names."

I spent the next ten minutes or so doing just that, and then I sent them to Courtney and Emily too, because they were always bugging me for puppy updates. I even emailed a few pictures to my mom, who was eager to know what I was up to in Vermont and more than ready for me to come home.

While I was sending out photos, Elizabeth, Blaze, Sunny, and Cherry curled up for a nap together. Violet put her head down and closed her eyes too. Before I was tempted to join them, I went down the hall to the kitchen. I got out my laptop and booted it up to check the job listings in Boston. So far, I'd applied for a dozen or so new positions, but I hadn't heard anything back, and I was starting to get worried.

I'd been here in Vermont for a week and a half already. I was behind on home renovations—thanks to Violet and her puppies—and I was burning through my savings at an alarming rate. But at the same time, I wasn't ready to go back to Boston, and not just because of the dogs in my bedroom. Despite my setbacks, I felt relaxed and happy here. At the end of the week, I would play my second set at V and V, and I was going out to dinner with Taylor beforehand.

Remembering her suggestion, I typed up a message introducing myself and offering my services as a financial consultant. It wasn't really my strong suit, but if the locals were willing to take a chance on me, it might help tide me over until I found a new full-time job.

My phone chimed with a new text message.

ADORABLE.

It was from Taylor, in response to the puppies' names.

Thanks, I replied. *Know any local Facebook groups where I could advertise my consulting services?*

I'll send you a list.

Well, that was promising. It would be a total game changer if I could find a way to cover my bills while I was here in Vermont. And since Taylor was helping me out, the least I could do was make good on my promise to her in return. I picked up my phone and dialed my dad.

"Hi, honey," he said in lieu of hello. "How are things in Vermont?"

"A little bit crazy," I admitted as a puppy squeal echoed down the hall. "Somehow, I got talked into fostering a mama dog and her puppies while I'm here."

"What in the world? How did that happen?" he asked.

"You remember Taylor Donovan, right?"

"Of course," he said. "You girls were best friends. If I had a dollar for every time I heard her name while you were growing up…"

"Right. Well, did you know she was keeping up Grandma's yard for us? Tending the rosebushes and all that?"

"No, I didn't," my dad said. "That was very nice of her."

"She and Grandma got pretty close these last few years, apparently."

"I do remember your grandma talking about her, now that you mention it," Dad said. "I think they walked their dogs together. But how did Taylor convince you to take in a litter of puppies?"

"She works at the shelter, and she was in a jam with this pregnant dog. Anyway, it's just for a few weeks while I'm here."

"Won't they pee all over the place?" Dad asked. "I can't rent out a cabin that smells like dog pee."

"I've got the laminate flooring in now, which should help, and I'll keep them confined in an area with pee pads if I'm still here when they get to that stage."

He sighed. "I don't like it. You should have talked to me about this before you agreed to it."

I rubbed my brow. "I'm sorry, Dad. It was a spur-of-the-moment thing."

"Is it too late to send them back?"

"Pretty sure it is," I told him.

"Do you want me to give the shelter a call? I'm sure I could convince someone to take those dogs back."

"No," I said quickly. I was twenty-nine years old, for crying out loud. When was my dad going to stop trying to fight my battles? "I agreed to this, and I'm going to see it through."

"Well, all right, but make sure they don't ruin anything."

"I'll be sure. Hey, I do have something to ask you, though," I said, remembering the reason for my call.

"Anything."

"I know you're pretty set on using the cabin as a rental property, but Taylor really wants to buy it. I just wanted to run it past you."

"It's not for sale," my dad responded automatically, as I'd known he would.

"I know, but just think about it, will you? She really loves this place, and it's right up the street from her parents' house. I know Grandma would have approved."

"You're probably right about that," Dad said. "But I want to keep it in the family so we can use it as a vacation home. I love that house too."

"Just think about it, please? It would really mean a lot to Taylor to have this place. I'm sure there are plenty of other rentals in the area you could stay in for a vacation."

"Okay," he said. "I'll think about it."

"Thanks, Dad. I appreciate it."

But when I ended the call a few minutes later, I didn't feel as happy as I should. When I looked around the living room with its newly gleaming laminate floors and roses blooming outside the windows, I felt a pang of regret.

Even if my dad agreed to sell, was I really ready to say goodbye to this house? Would I regret it if my family sold the cabin to Taylor?

18

TAYLOR

As I walked up the steps to Phoebe's front door on Friday evening, a funny tingle gripped my stomach. This felt uncomfortably like a date, and while I was looking forward to the chance to spend time with her and strengthen our newly rekindled friendship, I was awfully afraid these pesky sparks between us were going to be a problem before the end of the night.

I lifted my hand and knocked. From inside the house, I heard a bark and then the click of shoes on the floor as Phoebe approached the door. She opened it, wearing a knee-length purple dress and strappy black sandals. Her hair was down, and her eyes were wide.

"I think that's the first time I've heard Violet bark," she said. "And hi."

"Hi," I said. "It's a good sign, actually. It means she feels at home here now, like this is her territory to defend from intruders at the door."

"Oh." Phoebe looked down at Violet, who stood beside her, wagging her tail at me.

"Hi, Violet," I said as I stepped inside. She licked my hand when I reached out to pet her.

"I've already fed her, but I'm going to take her out for a quick walk before we leave," Phoebe said. "And I've already checked in with Holly to make sure she's all set. She'll be here in about an hour. I feel like a nervous new mom getting ready to leave my kids with a babysitter for the first time."

I smiled, enamored by this side of her, not to mention the enticing swell of cleavage in that dress when she bent over to fasten Violet's leash. "They'll be in great hands with Holly. I'm going to go see the puppies while you take her out."

Phoebe nodded, leading Violet toward the back door. I went down the hall to the bedroom where four furry pups were piled up against one side of the whelping area, fast asleep. The mostly white one—Sunny—was suckling in his sleep, paws twitching with puppy dreams.

I sat in front of the playpen, stroking them gently as they slept. God, they were cute. I could sit here and watch them for hours. Next to the pen was the notebook Phoebe was using to document their growth. I picked it up, smiling at her neat, blockish hand-writing. Not only had she recorded their weight twice a day since they were born, but she'd also created graphs for each puppy, illustrating their growth.

And as it turned out, I was a sucker for graphs, or at least I was a sucker for the woman who took the time to draw them for these tiny puppies. Each one showed a steady upward curve. They were just over a week old now and growing like weeds. Even Cherry, the littlest puppy who'd given us such a scare, seemed to be thriving.

I rubbed her, and she let out a squeak, rooting around as she looked for her mama. "She'll be back in just a minute," I told the puppy, even though she couldn't hear much yet. Her ears were still folded down against her head.

The back door clanged shut, and Violet's toenails clicked down the hall in my direction, followed by the tap of Phoebe's heels. Violet entered the bedroom first, stopping to greet me before she climbed in with her puppies. They squealed and squirmed as they snuggled against her, little bodies flailing with the effort.

When I looked up, Phoebe was standing in the doorway, one hand on her hip and a smile on her lips as she watched us. "Ready?" I asked, pressing my hands against my knees as I stood.

She nodded. "Where do you want to go for dinner?"

"There's a new farm-to-table restaurant not far from the bar, if you want to give that a try. I haven't been yet, but I've heard good things."

"Sounds perfect," she agreed.

I shoved my hands into my pockets to keep from reaching for one of her curls or touching any part of her, really. Her dress was loose and flowy, and I knew it would look amazing if she spun, but I wasn't taking her dancing tonight. Just dinner between friends. "You look really nice."

She ducked her head, giving me a shy smile. "Thanks. You look good too."

I was just wearing my usual Friday-night attire, black jeans and a T-shirt, but if I was being perfectly honest with myself, I'd spent a few more minutes in front of the mirror tonight than usual, wanting to look nice for Phoebe.

"Be a good girl until Holly gets here, okay?" Phoebe said, crouching to press a kiss against Violet's forehead. The dog's tail wagged against her bedding.

"She'll be fine," I assured her.

"I'm really excited for tonight," Phoebe said. "I'm used to going out to dinner with friends whenever I want, you know? I'm ready to get out of this house."

"Ready to go home?" I asked, pretending I didn't feel a little pang at the thought.

"Actually, no," she said. "I miss everyone so much, but things were such a mess when I left, and I don't want to deal with it yet. But I *am* excited for a night out in Burlington."

"I am too," I told her. "My life tends to revolve around the shelter, working with the animals, and my friends in the rescue community, but we don't go out for dinner or drinks very often."

"What about your friends at V and V?" Phoebe asked.

"I mostly just see them when I'm there on Fridays."

"Well, you should change that, then," Phoebe said as she grabbed her purse and led the way out the front door. "You should go out more often."

"I'll drive," I offered.

"Thanks." She walked toward the passenger door of my SUV.

"You're right. I do need to make more time for my social life, and I should try harder to date too. I guess I'm just a homebody at heart."

"You could try online dating," Phoebe suggested as she climbed into my SUV.

I settled in the driver's seat, doing my best not to look at her bare legs, smooth and tanned and just begging for me to reach over and touch. "I guess, but I really prefer to make a connection with someone in person."

"But how often does that actually happen?" Phoebe asked. "Online dating opens you up to a whole new world of available women, trust me. I've met most of my girlfriends that way."

"Maybe." I started the car and backed onto Mountain Laurel Road, headed toward downtown Burlington. "I'm sure the dating pool is wider in Boston."

"Well, of course," she said. "But there are plenty of queer women here in Vermont. Just look at the two of us."

"Right." But I didn't want to look at the two of us, because I already liked what I saw a little too much.

"Hey, I talked to my dad yesterday," she said, darting a glance at me.

"Yeah?"

"I pleaded your case for buying the house."

"You did?" I hadn't really expected her to follow through on that. Actually, I'd gotten the feeling that Phoebe didn't want to sell the cabin either. She seemed pretty fond of the place.

"I did," she confirmed. "But I have to warn you, he wasn't very receptive. He also wasn't thrilled about me having puppies in the house. But he did say he'd think about it."

"Well, that's something," I said, gripping the steering wheel a little bit tighter. "I really appreciate it, Phoebe." I'd been trying to quell my dreams about moving into Margery's cabin since it had seemed like a lost cause, but now…

"The least I could do," she said quietly.

"You'll miss it too, won't you?" I asked.

"I will," she said. "I love that house, but as you pointed out, I hardly ever make it up here to visit. You would make it a home, not a vacation house. Anyway, we'll see what my dad decides. Ultimately, it's his choice, not mine."

"Right," I said. "Fingers crossed." A small round shape in the road ahead caught my attention, and I tapped the brakes, pulling to the side of the road.

"What're you doing?" Phoebe asked, looking around.

"There's a turtle in the road," I told her. "I'm just going to give him a hand."

I climbed out of the car, looking both ways before I approached the turtle. It was a small painted turtle, one of the more common species around here, with a dark shell and the distinctive red and yellow marks on its neck that gave it its name. I lifted it carefully, gripping it about halfway down the shell so it couldn't try to bite me, but it immediately retracted inside its shell until I could just make out its little eyes staring warily at me.

"No worries, little dude," I said as I carried it to the far side of the road and set it down in the grass. "Enjoy the rest of your day."

I went back to the car, reaching into the backseat for one of the wipes I kept there to wash my hands. I worked with a lot of animals, and they tended to get messy, so I'd learned to be prepared.

"That was the most Taylor thing I've seen you do since I've been back, I think," Phoebe said, grinning at me.

I shrugged as I shifted the car into Drive and pulled back onto the road. "What can I say? I'm a sucker for animals in need."

"That you are. Why did you take it over there by the woods

instead of moving it toward that pond?" She gestured to the pond outside her window.

"You should always move them in the direction they were headed. He probably just came from the pond, so if I'd put him back on that side of the road, he'd have just crossed again."

"Ah," Phoebe said. "Good to know."

"I think this is their mating season, so he's probably off looking for a girl," I told her with a cheeky grin. "Or maybe it's a female looking for a place to lay her eggs."

"Well, at least the turtle's getting some," Phoebe said.

I snorted with laughter. "'Tis the season for wildlife to get frisky."

We shared easy conversation during the forty-minute drive into downtown Burlington. I parked in one of the public lots, and we walked to the restaurant, enjoying the cool evening breeze. To me, it felt crowded here. The street was lined with restaurants and shops, people bustling toward the pedestrian mall on Church Street. I could only take Burlington in small doses. Friday nights were plenty for me.

But Phoebe had a happy gleam in her eyes as she walked beside me, reminding me that she lived in the city. She liked the hustle and bustle of people, the noise, the crowds.

"I'm so happy to be out tonight," she said, and her fingers brushed mine as if she'd started to take my hand and then thought better of it.

"I'm glad," I told her. "And your energy is infectious."

She beamed at me. "It's been weeks since I've been out to dinner. I came to Vermont to hide out at my grandma's house, but I'm not really much of a recluse, I guess."

"No," I said. "You're a social butterfly. Always have been, always will be."

"You know what? You and I have never gone out to dinner together before," she said. "That's kind of hard to believe."

"We'd never shared a drink together until this month either," I reminded her. She'd been my best friend and my first love, but we'd been kids at the time. We'd never known each other as adults, and despite the challenge to my libido, I was glad we were getting the chance now. I stopped in front of the restaurant. "Here we are."

"Do you want to sit outside?" Phoebe asked, eyeing the outdoor patio, which was contained behind a wooden fence and decorated with a variety of hanging plants and strings of white lights. "It's so pretty."

"It sounds perfect," I told her. Fresh air was my natural element, after all.

The hostess led us to a small table in the back corner of the patio. We didn't have a good view of Church Street from here, but it was quiet, maybe even romantic...not that we were going for romantic tonight. A pink paper lantern hung above our table, and ivy ran down the brick wall beside it.

"I love it already," Phoebe said as she sank into the chair opposite me.

I was trying hard not to notice the way the breeze played through her hair as she reached for her menu. "Hope the food's as good as the ambience."

"I do too," she said.

I turned my attention to my own menu, perusing my options. The mushroom ravioli looked good, but it also sounded heavier than I was in the mood for tonight. Our waiter approached the table and introduced himself. Phoebe and I each ordered a beer and a plate of goat cheese with fruit and crackers as an appetizer to share.

"Oh my God," she said with a happy sigh as she continued to peruse the menu. "All this stuff is local? And it sounds so good. How have you not been here before?"

I shrugged. "I guess I don't go out to dinner that often."

"Well, I might drag you into town for a few more dinners before I leave, then," Phoebe said. "Because I love exploring new places, and you're basically the only person I know here."

"I'd like that," I said.

The waiter returned with our beer and cheese plate. Phoebe ordered a pork chop with various spring vegetables, and I got a seared steak salad. Once he'd gone, she gave me a thoughtful look.

"I have to say, I'm surprised you aren't a vegetarian, or a vegan even, being such an animal lover."

"I'm too pragmatic, I guess," I told her. "I don't have a problem with humanely sourced meat, but I do try to make sure everything I eat is locally and humanely raised."

"I respect that," she said. "I buy mostly organic myself, although local isn't as practical in Boston as it is here."

"No judgment from me. We all do what we can."

"Okay, I'm going in," she said, eyeing the cheese plate. She picked up a cracker, spread some goat cheese and raspberry sauce on it, and popped it in her mouth. Her eyes fluttered shut, and she gave an appreciative moan. "Mm, Taylor, you have to try this," she said once she'd swallowed.

I swallowed too, my throat gone dry as I watched her eat. I picked up my beer and took a hearty drink before fixing a cracker for myself. Flavor exploded across my tongue, the tangy cheese perfectly balanced by the sweetness of the fruit. "You're not wrong. This is amazing."

"If all the restaurants in Burlington are as good as this one, we're going to have go out to dinner a bunch of times," she said, loading up another cracker.

That sounded a lot like we were dating, but I supposed friends could go to dinner too. I wasn't going to press her on it, not while we were having such a nice evening together. "Oh yeah, who's going to watch your puppies?"

She looked up. "They'll get more self-sufficient, right?"

"They will for a little while, but then they take a step backward when they get big enough to eat and poop on their own."

Phoebe's nose wrinkled. "Let's not talk about poop at dinner."

I laughed. "Fair."

She took a drink of her beer and leaned back in her chair, a contented look on her face. "I really needed this night. And it doesn't seem like you Vermonters pay attention to online memes. No one's said anything to me since I got here."

"Did people actually stop you in the street?" I asked. "I mean, I don't think I'd recognize a person from a meme if I saw them in real life."

"Mostly people who knew me, I guess," she said. "Once word spread that it was *me* in the meme, it felt like everyone was talking about it. And if you know Boston, it's easy to tell where that photo was taken."

"Ah."

"I mean, to be fair, most people wanted to give me a fist bump and congratulate me on my badassery, but that meme imploded my life, so I didn't really feel like celebrating."

"Don't blame you."

"Someday, I'll appreciate it…maybe."

I grinned at her. "There are worse things to be known as than 'girl against the patriarchy,' that's for damn sure."

She lifted her beer and tapped it against mine. "I'll drink to that."

19

PHOEBE

I was in a happy haze by the time we left the restaurant, thanks in part to the two beers I'd had with dinner. The food had been amazing, and I was so happy to be back on good terms with Taylor. Right now, I was wondering how I'd gone through thirteen years of my life without her in it. How had I been such a coward that I'd let that happen?

"I have an hour before I need to start warming up for my set at V and V," I told her. "Want to walk along the waterfront?"

"I'd love that. It's about a ten-minute walk from here, though. Are your shoes comfortable?"

I nodded. "They're very comfortable."

Taylor gave my sandals a skeptical look, but they only had a one-inch heel, and they were truly some of the most comfortable shoes I owned. "Let's go, then."

We walked down Main Street toward Waterfront Park. It was a welcome splash of green among all the bricks and cement, with tree-lined walking paths and a boardwalk, which was where Taylor led me. Before us, Lake Champlain glistened against the sunset, as wide and vast as the ocean, from this vantage point, at least. Gentle waves slapped the shore, and a vee of geese glided by overhead.

"Gorgeous," I proclaimed.

"Doesn't compare to Boston, I bet," Taylor said.

"We do have some nice harbor views, but this has a different charm." I rested my arms on the wooden railing, gazing out over the water. "It doesn't look the same as the ocean. The water's greener, and it smells different, although my mind boggles at a lake this big."

"It's nice. I guess I sometimes forget I live so close to one of the Great Lakes. My life tends to revolve around the forest instead."

"Maybe you should make time for the lake too. Can you take a boat out on it?" I asked, glancing toward the marina, where neat rows of boats were moored.

"I'm sure you can, but I have no idea how."

"Maybe we should find out while I'm here."

"Maybe," Taylor said. She was staring out at the water, her expression distant.

I couldn't quite read her vibe right now. We'd had such a nice dinner, friendly and relaxed, but now she seemed to be pulling back. I didn't think it was anything I'd said. Maybe she just felt like she needed some boundaries with me, lest we get carried away like we had the night the puppies were born.

I wasn't the only one who still felt the tug of attraction between us. I'd seen her check out my dress earlier tonight and the way her gaze occasionally lingered on my breasts. We were both feeling it, but surely people could be friends with someone they were attracted to. It must happen all the time. And if things got out of hand, I could always head back to Boston early.

Or stay in Vermont a bit longer. I'd gotten a call that morning from a woman in town, asking for my financial advice after she'd seen my post in the local Facebook group. If I got enough of those calls, I might be able to stay until the puppies were weaned. In fact, as I stood at this windswept railing beside Taylor, I hoped I got that chance.

"We should head back soon, so you're not late for your set," she said, glancing at me.

"Yep." I stared at her, mesmerized by the way the fading sun played through the russet layers of her hair and gleamed in her eyes. The pull between us was almost magnetic. I leaned toward her before I'd even realized what I was doing.

Her gaze sharpened, and she took a step back, returning the necessary space between us to keep me from being a big fraud. Just friends. Right. I could do this. *We* could do this.

She turned away from the railing, leading the way down the boardwalk toward the path where we'd entered the park. My heels tapped rhythmically against the wooden boards as I walked, a sharper sound than the thump of her boots. I liked the way they went together, like music.

I'd been thinking about music a lot since I got to Vermont, remembering the way it used to call to me. I liked the evenness of it, the rhythmic beats, counting bars and verses. It made sense in the math side of my brain. And right now, our shoes were making a perfect melody together.

As we made our way through the marketplace, crowded with locals and tourists enjoying their Friday evening, nerves began to tingle in my belly. I had enjoyed playing in the bar earlier this month, and I knew I would again tonight, but I wasn't used to performing in public. It still made my palms sweat, even though I was looking forward to it.

"Hey, before we go in, do you mind if we find a quiet place to sit for a minute so I can do some vocal warm-ups?" I asked.

Taylor smiled at me. "Sure. I know a place."

She led me down a little alley behind the bar where it was much quieter, then leaned back, propping one of her feet against the wall as she settled in to watch me warm up. Speaking of warming up, my cheeks were pretty hot beneath her appraising gaze. I closed my eyes and ran through a few scales to prepare my voice. My throat was dry, though. I'd need to ask for a glass of water at the bar before I sang.

"Okay," I said when I'd finished, opening my eyes. "I'm ready."

"You have a really pretty voice," she said. "Do you still think about singing professionally?"

I shook my head. "Thank you, but I don't want anything more than what I'm doing here at V and V. Nothing about fame appeals to me, and I don't think my voice is *that* good, anyway. It's just something I enjoy as a hobby."

"Fair enough," she said.

We walked to the front of Vino and Veritas together, and Taylor opened the door for me. To our right was the bookstore, and the wine bar was to the left. As we entered the bar, I asked Taylor, "Have you ever shopped at the bookstore?"

She shook her head. "It's usually closed by the time I get here. I'd like to, though."

"Me too. I love supporting local bookstores. Maybe we can stop in together sometime." My gaze fell on the stage, and another burst of nerves gripped my stomach.

Taylor grabbed my hand. "You got this, Phoebs."

"Thanks." I smiled at her, warmed by what I saw in her eyes. I approached the counter to check in with Molly, the auburn-haired bartender who'd served me the first time I came in. She brought me a glass of water, and then I settled myself at the piano on the little stage in the corner. When I looked over my shoulder, Taylor was at the bar with a glass of her favorite cider in hand.

I returned my gaze to the piano and warmed up with a few simple bars, letting my fingers roam the keys the way my grandma had taught me. I didn't realize what song I'd chosen until I looked up and saw Taylor's eyes boring into mine.

I was playing our song.

Two hours later, I stood from the piano to a smattering of cheers and claps. It wasn't overwhelming, but to me, it felt perfect. I wasn't looking for fame. I was looking for fun, and tonight, I'd found it. I'd enjoyed every moment on that stage, especially the way Taylor watched me from the bar, like she couldn't take her eyes off me.

In fact, it had been hard to keep my eyes off her too.

I made my way toward her now, pausing to talk to Molly on the way. By the time I made it to the bar, Taylor had a glass of white wine sitting next to her cider. She pushed it toward the empty stool beside her, gesturing for me to sit.

"Is that for me?" I asked.

She nodded. "Figured you'd be ready for a drink."

"Thank you," I told her. It was a little thing—buying me a drink—but little things added up to become big things, and my feelings for Taylor had been building since I arrived in Vermont. I lifted the glass and sipped, recognizing the chardonnay I'd had last time.

"You sounded good up there," she said, sliding a glance at me.

"Thanks. It felt good. I really enjoy it." I took another sip of wine. One of my favorite things about white wine was the contrast between the cool liquid as I swallowed with the warmth it created inside me.

"A lot has changed since we were here two weeks ago," Taylor said.

I laughed, swirling the stem of my wineglass between my fingertips to watch the lights play through its golden depths. "It feels like a lifetime ago."

"It really does."

"I'm glad for everything that's happened since," I said. "Every moment."

Taylor inhaled as my words hung between us. I hadn't been thinking about our kiss when I said it, but I was now. So was she, if her dazed expression was any indication. Her gaze dropped to my lips, and it was my turn to suck in a breath.

She was the one who leaned in this time, but I met her halfway. Our lips brushed together, and just like last time, she tasted like apple cider. I was developing a thing for it, or at least for the taste of it on Taylor's lips. I rested a hand on her jean-clad thigh as my lips explored hers. My eyes slid shut as I lost myself in the kiss, absorbing the pleasure of her mouth and the way it made my body tingle from my scalp to my toes.

After a long minute, we parted, both of us breathing hard as we sat up on our stools. "Wow."

"Yeah." She stared at me, blinking rapidly, like she didn't know what to say. Maybe she didn't know how she felt about our kiss. I wasn't sure I did either, but I couldn't bring myself to regret it.

I reached for my wine to give myself something to do. I wanted to tell her that we should quit fighting this chemistry and just go for it, that we should drown ourselves in each other for the rest of my time in Vermont and see what happened. But, for any number of reasons, that might not be the best idea. I didn't want to hurt Taylor when I left, and I didn't want to get hurt either.

I was barely out of my relationship with Sabrina, and my feelings for Taylor were already deep and complicated. In the end, I polished off my glass of wine while she drank the rest of her cider, and we left the bar in an uncomfortable web of silence. It grew with every step as we crossed the marketplace toward the lot where Taylor's SUV was parked.

"Holly texted while I was playing," I said finally, desperate to get some conversation going. I couldn't bear for our evening to end on this awkward note. "She said Violet and the puppies are fine. She stayed with them about an hour."

"Good," Taylor said. "I'm glad she was able to stop by."

"I had a really great time tonight," I couldn't help saying.

"I did too." But she didn't look at me as she clicked the lock on the car. The lights flashed, and we each went around to our doors and climbed inside.

"And thanks for driving," I added.

"Any time. I know these roads at night a lot better than you do."

"That's true." I relaxed into my seat. After a week that had revolved almost entirely around a litter of puppies, it had been good to go out tonight. Everything about my life since I got to Vermont was unrecognizable to what my life in Boston was like, but I kind of liked it this way. I'd needed a change of pace, and I'd definitely found one here.

We were mostly quiet during the drive home, but it was a different kind of silence. This one felt comfortable. We were both tired after a long evening, although there was still an undercurrent of tension running between us. To me, it felt like a "what's going to happen when we get to my house" kind of tension. Would Taylor come in to check on the puppies? And if she did, would we kiss again? Would she stay?

Did I want her to?

I did. Maybe it wasn't smart, but I still wanted her, and I was tired of fighting it. Maybe we owed it to ourselves to find out what would happen if we gave this thing between us a real chance. Maybe we'd implode. Maybe we'd find something worth fighting for. The only thing I knew for sure was that I'd regret not finding out.

Taylor turned her SUV into my driveway. The windows in the master bedroom and the kitchen gleamed brightly in the darkness. Holly must have left the lights on when she visited. Gravel crunched beneath the tires as Taylor pulled in behind my car and cut the engine.

I looked at her, but she was staring straight ahead. "Do you, um, do you want to come in?"

She hesitated long enough for me to wonder if I was the only one ready to make the leap from friends to lovers. When she looked at me, I felt a punch of adrenaline somewhere in the vicinity of my diaphragm, making my lungs expand as I gulped air.

Her nod was barely perceptible in the dim interior of the SUV. "Yes."

20

TAYLOR

My heart beat frantically as I followed Phoebe into the house. Tonight could go any number of ways, and it was probably up to me to decide what happened next. Phoebe had been quiet since our kiss, letting me take the lead, but she'd also invited me in. She'd launched the ball into my court. I just wasn't sure what I wanted to do with it yet.

Violet greeted us at the front door, tail wagging so vigorously that it shook her whole body from side to side. I hadn't seen her this animated before. She was blooming in Phoebe's care, just like the roses out back and the puppies in the bedroom, while my self-control was withering.

"I'm going to take her outside," Phoebe said.

"Good idea. I'll check on the puppies." I went down the hall to the bedroom, where the puppies were in a sleepy pile much as they had been when we left. I sat by the pen and rubbed them, loving the warm, soft feel of their fur beneath my fingers and the way they wiggled, feet flailing as they adjusted their positions.

While I waited for Phoebe to come back inside, I went into the guest bathroom to freshen up, and then I walked to the kitchen for a glass of water. I gulped most of it without stopping.

"Good idea," Phoebe said as she stepped through the back

door, unclipping Violet's leash. The dog trotted over for a drink of her own while Phoebe joined me by the sink to pour herself a glass.

Violet looked up at us and whined before giving her empty food bowl a pointed look.

"Real subtle, Vi," Phoebe said with a giggle. "I guess it's time for your midnight snack."

"Nursing mama's got to eat," I agreed, and my chest got all warm and gooey as I watched Phoebe prepare a bowl for Violet, expertly mixing the wet and dry puppy chow to fix her a high-calorie meal. She placed the bowl on the floor, and Violet dove right in, scarfing down her food.

"She's such a good girl," Phoebe said, giving the dog an affectionate look.

And that did it. I set my glass on the counter and pulled her in for a kiss. She gasped in surprise, eyes going wide before she wrapped her arms around me and kissed me back. This was different from the other times we'd kissed. This time, I wasn't going to pull back after a minute and go home, and we both knew it.

Maybe there had never been any other possible outcome for us, because as her tongue slid into my mouth, crisp and cool as the glass of water she'd just drank, this felt indescribably *right*. I couldn't let her go back to Boston without knowing what it would be like with her now that we were adults, and if my heart was going to get broken, at least it would break after I'd learned all the secrets of her body that I hadn't gotten to explore when we were sixteen.

Beside us, Violet finished her dinner and wandered down the hall toward her puppies. Phoebe and I kept kissing. I pressed her against the counter as I sank my hands into her hair, reacquainting myself with its soft depths.

"God, I missed this," I murmured, and she smiled against my lips.

"To me, it feels brand-new." Her breath fanned across my cheeks.

I slid my hands down her back, settling them at the curve of her waist. "How so?" Because to me, her kiss was a homecoming.

"I was *so* naïve the last time we were together," she said, gasping as I bent my head to place a kiss against the hollow of her throat. "I'd never been kissed before. I didn't even know for sure yet that I was gay. I was just clueless about myself in general, so I guess I was always holding back."

"And now?"

"I'm not so innocent anymore," she whispered, angling her head so I could continue kissing her neck. "And I'm not holding anything back."

"Nothing?" I asked, warmth blooming in my core at the thought.

"Nothing."

I swirled my tongue over the pulse point on her neck before venturing down to her collarbone, fascinated by every inch of exposed skin. Phoebe whimpered, spreading her thighs so I could settle myself between them. She was right about one thing. She hadn't been this bold in high school. Neither of us had been.

We owed it to ourselves to satisfy the need, the curiosity, the longing that had lingered between us since that summer. Maybe once we satisfied it, we could part ways unscathed. Probably not, but who knew? Maybe sex with Phoebe would be under-whelming.

But as she clamped her thighs around mine, I knew that wouldn't be the case. I was already so turned on, I could hardly stand it.

"Taylor," she whispered.

"Yeah?"

"Let's not do this in the kitchen."

I pressed my face against the warm skin of her neck as laughter gripped me, and when I raised my head, she had her bottom lip pinched between her teeth, eyes sparkling with amusement—and heat—as they met mine. "Lead the way."

She put her hands on my chest and stepped me backward so she could slip past me, grabbing my hand as we walked down the hall. When we reached the master bedroom, though, she took one look at the whelping pen in the corner and tugged me into the guestroom instead. "Change of plans."

"Don't want Violet to watch?" I asked.

"She's nosy, and puppy noises aren't sexy."

"All true, and maybe even more importantly, do you know how many times I fantasized about having my way with you on this very bed?" I asked as I nudged her toward the twin bed with the blue-striped quilt that we'd spent so many, *many* hours on as teenagers.

"How many?" she asked as her hands found the hem of my T-shirt and slipped beneath.

"*Too* many."

Her fingers gripped my hips as she pressed her body against mine. I nudged her backward until she sat on the bed, and then I followed her down, laying her flat on the quilt as I lowered myself on top of her. She was so warm and soft beneath me, breasts pressing against mine. It was so much like our teenage make-out sessions, but not, because tonight, there was no reason to stop.

"Taylor?" she murmured, shifting beneath me so that my knee slid into the space between hers, my jeans pressed against her bare skin.

"Yes?"

"I want you to know, this isn't just a rebound for me or a fling before I go back to Boston. I'm here with you tonight because this feels right." She stared straight into my eyes as she spoke, and there went my traitorous heart again, melting hopelessly for this woman.

"It feels right to me too." I had no idea what the future held for us, but tonight felt inevitable.

Phoebe pulled me down so she could kiss me, and this time,

neither of us held anything back. Her tongue danced with mine, hot and intoxicating, igniting every cell in my body with the over-powering sense of need I always seemed to feel with her. This was more than just sex because it was with Phoebe.

I propped myself on my left elbow, resting my right hand on her bare knee as we kissed. Slowly, I slid my hand up her thigh, eliciting a shiver from Phoebe. I could feel the goose bumps on her skin under my fingers, but I didn't think she was cold if the warmth radiating from her skin was any indication.

My hand slid beneath her dress, coming to rest on her hip where a thin band of lace met my fingertips. Tonight, I would get to see all of her, and I was half drunk on anticipation. Phoebe reached for the hem of my T-shirt, and I sat up to help her lift it over my head, baring the simple black bra I wore beneath. She cupped my breasts, thumbs skimming back and forth over my nipples.

I groaned, lowering my hips so that I was straddling her thigh. She brought her hands from my breasts to my hips, encouraging me to move against her. Arousal burned inside me, a pleasure so exquisite that I wanted this moment to last forever, and at the same time, I wanted to rip off all our clothes so I could have my way with her as quickly as possible.

I settled on something in the middle, leaning forward to explore her dress while I kissed her senseless. Our kisses grew sloppier with every passing minute, Phoebe's hips shifting rest-lessly beneath mine as she sought friction. I brought my thigh against her, giving her what she needed, and she rocked against me with a breathy moan.

"God, you feel good." She drew me closer, our hips shifting together.

"Mm, so do you." I kissed my way down to that sensitive spot just above her collarbone that had always reduced her to a quiv-ering mess, but tonight, I didn't have to leave her all hot and both-ered the way I had at sixteen. Tonight, I wanted to blow her mind.

Repeatedly.

"God, Taylor," she moaned, arching her hips so that her core pressed against me, and I could feel her heat through my jeans.

"Can I?" I asked, gripping the purple fabric of her dress between my fingers.

"Please," she said, lifting her hips off the mattress to help me remove her dress.

I slid it past her waist, revealing lavender lace panties that were impossibly sexy and feminine and so Phoebe. She'd always been a girly-girl. I helped her wiggle the rest of the way out of her dress, baring a matching bra, because of *course* she wore a matching set.

I'd never owned matching underwear in my life, and I while could choose to think she'd worn this set just for me, I suspected she always dressed like this beneath her clothes. One thing I hadn't expected, though, was the little bird tattooed on her right hip. I bent my head to kiss it, watching as goose bumps pebbled her skin again. "When did you get this?"

"When I was twenty-three, right after I came out," she said, and I could feel her chest rising and falling beneath me as she gulped for breath. "It reminded me of my time here in Vermont, the way the birds would fly overhead when we lay in our field together, like they didn't have a care in the world. They were free, and so was I."

My throat constricted at this unexpected insight into Phoebe's psyche. "I'm so glad you found that kind of freedom."

"I'm just sorry it took me so long," Her voice had grown hoarse, as if she were fighting emotions of her own.

"Everyone has their own path and their own pace," I told her before circling her tattoo with my tongue. I could almost taste her freedom in the salty flavor of her skin.

"I was so envious of you," she said quietly. "You knew exactly who you were and what you wanted when we were sixteen."

"*You* were what I wanted then, and you still are."

In response, Phoebe reached for the button on my jeans. She popped it open and pushed down the zipper. I sat back, letting her help me wiggle out of my jeans. Then we were both in our underwear, bodies pressed together as electricity crackled between us. It seemed to scorch my fingers where I touched her, burning me with the strength of our chemistry.

We scrambled out of our underwear, and my hungry gaze fell to Phoebe's exposed breasts, so small and perfect. Every inch of her was perfect, and I couldn't wait another moment. I dropped my head to her breast, nipping and kissing as I brought my hand between her thighs, encountering her slick wetness.

Phoebe gasped, flinging an arm across her eyes as she arched her back, pressing herself more firmly against me. I kissed my way across her breasts, paying attention to every gorgeous inch until her nipples had hardened into tight peaks and her hips were grinding against my hand as a steady string of needy noises escaped her throat.

I scooted down so I could kiss my way over her belly, desperate to taste her. I'd been waiting thirteen years for this moment.

"Oh my God, Taylor," she panted, burying her hands in my hair.

I positioned one of her legs to rest over my shoulder as I pressed my tongue against her. I tenderly kissed my way over her folds, acquainting myself with her body and which spots brought the loudest cries from her throat. I dipped my tongue inside her, drunk on the sharp taste of her and the way her muscles clamped down on me, seeking more.

Her hips moved rhythmically against me, her fingers tangled deeply in my hair. I moved up to flick my tongue against her clit, and she let out a sharp cry. I swirled my tongue there, empowered by her responsiveness and the knowledge that this was *Phoebe*. A few more strokes of my tongue, and she let out a breathy groan as she came against my mouth.

I held myself still as she rode out her release, and then I kissed my way up her body to her mouth. She clamped her arms around me, holding me close while she caught her breath.

"Jesus, Taylor," she gasped, kissing me between rapid breaths. "You're really freaking good at that."

I just grinned at her, ridiculously pleased by her praise and also ridiculously aroused from getting her off. I could feel my own wetness slicking my thighs, and the ache in my core burned relentlessly beneath Phoebe's heated gaze.

The next thing I knew, she'd flipped us. My back met the soft fabric of the quilt as she pressed her lithe body over me like a warm blanket. I closed my eyes, surrendering to her touch, desperate for it. She took her time at first, touching and kissing every inch of my chest until I was ready to beg for more.

When she sucked my nipple into the delicious heat of her mouth, my hips bucked off the bed and an embarrassingly loud moan escaped my lips. The thing was, I didn't even care. Right now, I was putty beneath Phoebe's talented fingers, and *oh*, her fingers were talented. After stroking her way down my belly, she slid her hand between my thighs. Her fingers moved deftly, exploring my body, and within minutes, she had me spiraling toward the point of no return.

She plunged two fingers inside me, curling them forward as her thumb caressed my clit, and I was flying. Release radiated out from my core and sizzled through my blood, leaving me boneless and breathless beneath her, sparks still pinging through my body.

"Wow," I whispered when I could form words.

Phoebe grinned down at me, those chestnut curls hanging around her face in disarray, the most beautiful thing I'd ever seen. "Wow doesn't even begin to cover it."

21

PHOEBE

"Will you stay?" I whispered into the depths of Taylor's hair. I had no idea what time it was, except that it was late. After several rounds of sweaty sex, we were tangled up together in my bed, exhausted in the very best way.

"I wish I could," she murmured, trailing a hand up and down my spine. "But I need to get home to my dogs. They've been alone since about six."

"I wish yours got along with mine so you could just bring them with you next time."

"Next time?" Her eyes burned into mine in the moonlit bedroom.

"I hope there's a next time," I said. "Don't you?"

"Yeah," she admitted. "And it's not that they wouldn't get along. Violet's good with other dogs. She just might get protective of her puppies, and I don't want to stress her out while they're small. Once they're older, she'd probably be fine with Minnie coming over."

"Just Minnie?" I asked.

"Well, Blue's shy, but also hopefully he'll be adopted soon."

"Right." I wasn't as familiar with fostering as she was. The whole process seemed confusing and a little bit upsetting to me.

The idea of giving up a dog after you'd helped them overcome whatever trauma had led them to the shelter seemed emotionally difficult, and Taylor did it over and over. "Can you stay a little while longer?"

"Yeah." Her arms tightened around me. "I'd like that."

"Want to raid my fridge?" I asked. "Because I seem to have worked up an appetite."

She giggled, and the sound energized me, like someone had just put my battery on the charger. "Let's do it."

We disentangled ourselves and climbed out of bed. I gave her one of my T-shirts to wear, and she went into the guest bath across the hall to freshen up while I ducked into the master bath, pausing to check on Violet, who was fast asleep with her puppies.

Taylor and I met up in the kitchen, where we poured fresh glasses of water and went through my fridge, looking for a midnight snack. I pulled out a bag of carrot sticks and a bottle of dip while Taylor reached for a jar of pickles. We munched on veggies and chased them with a handful of Oreos, because why not?

Then we snuggled under my grandma's quilt in the master bed, watching Violet and the puppies. My legs were entwined with hers, and I wondered how something could feel so comfortable, so familiar, when we'd only been together, *really* together, for a few hours.

"Remember when we were little and we'd go wading in the stream out back?" she asked, one hand playing idly with my hair. She twirled one of my curls around her finger, watching as it sprang free in a tight ringlet.

"You told me there were crayfish in the water, and I was terrified the whole time that one was going to bite my toes."

She laughed. "Yep. You bumped your foot on a rock and shrieked like you were being attacked by a bear. Margery came running out of the house expecting something awful."

"Totally your fault," I told her. "You made me paranoid."

"We had a lot of fun during our summer vacations together."

"We sure did." I pinched her ass beneath the blankets. "I never saw it leading here."

"Neither did I," she said. "Or at least, certainly not back when we were splashing in the stream together."

"When did you?" I hadn't seen Taylor as anything but a friend until shortly before our first kiss, after she'd come out and awakened in me the idea that I might not be straight either.

"Do you really want to know?" she asked, suddenly serious.

"Yes," I answered immediately, and then I had a moment of panic wondering how long she'd had feelings for me. Was it much longer than my own?

"The summer we were fourteen," she answered quietly.

"Oh," I blurted. "Really?"

"Yep." She looked away, her body tensing slightly beneath my fingers.

"Tell me," I implored. Fourteen? I'd been particularly miserable that summer. My parents were fighting nonstop, and they'd each called me repeatedly, asking uncomfortable questions about the other. Apparently, I'd been too caught up in my family drama to notice what was happening with Taylor.

"You were my first crush," she whispered. "You were my best friend, and suddenly, I was fantasizing about kissing you. It was a very confusing summer."

"Why didn't you say anything?" I asked, dumbfounded.

"I was terrified of ruining our friendship. At the time, the idea that you might be gay too seemed inconceivable. I didn't even know for sure yet that I was gay. I thought it might just be a phase. Maybe all girls fantasized about kissing their best friend."

Now it was my turn to laugh. "That's exactly how I felt two summers later, after you came out to me. I started to fantasize about kissing *you* and wondered all the same things."

"And here we are." She brushed a hand through my hair.

"I know you need to go home soon, but will you come back tomorrow?" I asked. "I'd love to spend some of our Saturday together."

"I can do that," she said, but there was something hesitant in her tone, like she wasn't sure how to approach a relationship with me. I knew she was afraid of getting hurt, because I was too.

"Well, I'll be around all day, just hanging out with Violet and getting some things done around the house. I'm going to try to get all the trim painted this weekend."

"Okay. Would you mind if I bring Minnie and Blue and we go for a hike together? Violet should be fine by herself for a few hours."

"Sure. Bring them," I agreed. Unspoken between us was fact that we needed to talk. We needed to sit down in the light of day and figure out what happened next. Were we going to try to make a real go of this, or were we just having some fun together while I was in Vermont?

"It's a date, then." She rolled toward me, giving me a kiss. "And I need to get going, before I get too tired to drive home."

"Right." I was pretty damn tired myself. The urge to stay right here beside her and sleep was strong. Instead, I tossed the quilt back and crawled out of bed.

Taylor went into the guest bedroom to gather her clothes, reappearing a minute later to kiss me good night. "I'll give you a call in the morning."

I nodded. "Or just show up if you want. I'm not going anywhere tomorrow."

"Okay." And with that, she was gone.

I stood in the living room, watching the lights from her SUV as she backed out of my driveway and drove away. And then I stood there for another minute, just replaying our evening together in my mind, because holy shit. It had all been so amazingly perfect, and now I wasn't sure what to think or how to feel. Could we find a way to make this work?

The telltale click of toenails against the laminate floors announced Violet's arrival. She wandered into the kitchen, licked my leg, and walked to her water bowl for a drink.

"You probably need to go out again before I go to bed, don't you?" I asked her.

She looked up with that solemn face, but her tail was wagging. I clipped her leash to her collar, and she led the way down the stairs into the backyard. It was cooler outside now, cold enough to make me shiver as I stood at the bottom of the stairs. While I waited for Violet, I looked up at the canopy of stars overhead. It never ceased to amaze me how many stars you could see here in Vermont.

Violet was always quick about her business late at night. She peed and headed right back up the steps. I followed her in, locking the door behind me before bending to unclip her leash. I went into the bathroom to brush my teeth and wash up, and by the time I came back out, she was asleep in her pen with the puppies. Since they were still annoyingly noisy during the night, I went into the guest room and curled up in the bed I'd so recently shared with Taylor. Smiling, I closed my eyes and slipped into a deep, peaceful sleep.

When I woke, sunlight streamed through the thin lacy curtains over my window. I stretched, smiling as I remembered last night. My body was sore in all the right places, satisfaction still swimming in my veins. As I climbed out of bed, I saw that Violet wasn't up yet, so I took the opportunity to step into a quick shower.

From there, I fixed breakfast and weighed the puppies. They were all growing nicely, even little Cherry. She wriggled in my hands, so warm and soft. Her eyes were still closed, but even so, she looked much more puppy-ish than she had when she was born. They all did. They'd be running all over the place in no time, and while that was exhausting and annoying to think about, I couldn't really be upset about it either, because they were so cute.

Actually, I was looking forward to seeing what their little faces looked like once their eyes were open and all the mayhem they caused when they started running around. It was only for a few weeks.

I held Cherry up in front of me. Her head was almost entirely white, which meant the skin on her nose and around her ears was as pink as the rose she was named after. But maybe my favorite part of her—and all the puppies—was her belly. She was so round, like she'd swallowed an orange, except this particular belly was full of milk.

I stroked her for a minute, talking gently to her. Taylor said I should be holding and talking to them every day to get them used to being handled and to keep Violet from getting overprotective. She'd been great so far, though. She was completely chill about me holding her babies. I liked to think we'd developed a mutual trust.

Once I was finished with the puppies, I changed into an old T-shirt and jean cutoffs and tied my hair back to get to work. The new baseboards I'd installed needed painting. Even though Violet's arrival had slowed me down, I'd still gotten a lot done in the two and a half weeks I'd been here. The renovations were almost finished, which meant I could start shopping for décor and knickknacks to turn this place into a vacation retreat. And since my dad was footing the bill, I was really, *really* looking forward to going shopping.

I finished painting the trim in the living room and had started working my way down the hall toward the bedrooms when I heard a knock at the door. Violet hopped out of her bed, dislodging several puppies who had been nursing. They howled their displeasure as she trotted down the hall, barking.

"It's just Taylor," I told her as I followed her.

Violet raced to the front door and stood there, her body tense and alert as she barked, waiting to see if friend or foe was on the other side of the door. I was on high alert too, but for different reasons. A happy thrill raced through me at the prospect of seeing Taylor again, along with a healthy dose of nerves, because what if it was awkward?

What if she regretted last night? There was plenty of room for regret since I was only here temporarily, and neither of us wanted to get hurt. Maybe I was still basking in the adrenaline rush of last night, but I didn't regret a single moment. I opened the door to reveal Taylor standing there wearing a black backpack.

"I packed lunch," she said. "But do you mind if we take it to go? I've got my dogs, so I thought we could make a picnic in the woods, if that sounds good."

"I'd love that. Give me just a minute to put my shoes on and get Violet squared away."

At the sound of her name, she poked her head around my legs, tail wagging as she caught sight of Taylor. Taylor stooped to pet her, and Violet licked her face enthusiastically.

"I've got everything we need in my backpack," Taylor told me. "Just bring yourself."

"Easy enough. Thank you." I wanted to give her a quick kiss, but I wasn't sure yet what the new parameters of our relationship would be, so I held myself back. Instead, I went inside to close the can of trim paint and change out of my paint-spattered T-shirt. A few minutes later, I headed out back to meet Taylor.

She was already down by the stream with Minnie and Blue. I felt myself smiling as I walked toward them, and Minnie came bounding in my direction, tongue out and filled with that effervescent enthusiasm she seemed to have in endless supply.

"Hey, Minnie," I said as she reached me. "I missed you too."

Minnie sniffed my legs as her tail swished, probably checking out the competition since she and Violet hadn't met yet. I rubbed behind her ears, and my fingers snagged in her thick, fluffy fur. I'd forgotten just how shaggy she was, having gotten used to Violet's sleek coat. After greeting her, I crossed the wooden bridge toward the hiking trail, where Taylor stood waiting with Blue at her side.

He reminded me a little bit of Violet with that quiet personality, but she was starting to come out of her shell now. She barked and spun in happy circles in the kitchen while I was making her food. I wondered if Blue would always be this solemn or if he came out of his shell too when he was at home with Taylor.

"A picnic lunch is an unexpected treat," I said as I joined her, leaning in for a quick kiss before I could stop myself.

She kissed me back, reaching up to tug at a curl of my hair before she led the way onto the path. "I thought it would be fun, and these guys really need a hike."

I laughed as Minnie dropped a stick at my feet. I really had created a monster where she was concerned. "Where are we headed? The gazebo?"

Taylor looked over her shoulder at me. "Actually, I thought we could spread out a blanket in our field."

22

TAYLOR

I opened my backpack and took out the large plaid blanket I'd packed. Phoebe grabbed one side of it, helping me unfold it, but as we held it between us, Minnie dashed underneath, nipping at the fabric from below. "Minnie," I chastised. "We aren't playing a game. Go on."

She darted out from under the blanket and grabbed her stick. We spread the blanket on the ground, and Minnie promptly leaped onto it, still carrying her stick.

"She's enthusiastic. I'll give her that," Phoebe said as she sat on the blanket and gave Minnie a rub.

"She sure is." I sat beside her.

Phoebe picked up Minnie's stick and tossed it with a smile. The sun caught in her hair, making it glisten. Around us, the field was a dappled mixture of green and brown, with a smattering of red, purple, and yellow from the wildflowers that bloomed here.

This had always been one of my favorite places. I brought my dogs here often, but it felt so different today with Phoebe. Memories hung heavy in the air. When we'd laid on a blanket here together as teenagers, daydreaming about what our futures held, I doubted either of us had imagined this moment.

"Hungry?" I asked.

Phoebe nodded, turning her gaze on me. I'd thought she was gorgeous last night in her purple dress at V and V, but right now, in her tank top and shorts with no makeup and bathed in sunshine, she was the most beautiful woman in the world.

I opened the backpack and started pulling out containers of food. I'd packed us a snack lunch, my favorite kind of picnic. We had cheese, crackers, pepperoni, grapes, olives, and some chocolate chip cookies I'd bought at the store.

"This looks amazing," Phoebe said.

I produced paper plates and bottles of water, and we started to eat. She sat cross-legged across from me, rolling a pepperoni around a piece of cheese like a funny little burrito. "I've never seen anyone eat it that way before," I said as I stacked a piece of cheese and a pepperoni on top of a cracker.

"It's good. You should try it."

"I'll take your word for it," I told her as I ate my cracker.

Minnie crawled between us, looking from Phoebe to me with her most pleading expression. Blue sat beside me, watching us with his head resting between his front paws. Phoebe slipped a covert pepperoni to Minnie before giving me a sheepish look, and I rolled my eyes. Generally, I toed a hard line when it came to feeding human food to my dogs, but I seemed to be soft where Phoebe was concerned.

We snacked and chatted until all the food was gone. I packed up our trash, and we lay on the blanket together. Minnie snuggled beside me, her furry head resting against my thigh. Blue lay at the edge of the blanket, preferring his own space. His leash was looped around my wrist for safekeeping.

"It looks so much the same," Phoebe said, sliding her hand into mine. "And yet, so different."

"More dogs?" I teased. Occasionally, we'd brought Margery's dog Comet with us as teenagers, but usually it had been just the two of us.

"There's that, but maybe it's just that I *feel* different. I used to be so worried someone would see us. I was terrified my family would find out about us and what they'd say. It was exhausting trying to keep myself hidden."

"How did they take it when you came out?" I asked.

"A lot better than I'd feared," she said. "My dad went outside to work in the yard while he processed it, and my mom got really awkward and talked too much. But neither of them said anything awful, and after they'd gotten over the shock, they both told me they loved and supported me. It took them a while to get used to seeing me with another woman, but they came around eventually."

"I'm glad."

"Do you ever think about the fact that no one who knew us then knows we were together?" Phoebe asked.

"One person knew," I told her.

She rolled toward me, fingertips trailing up and down my arm. "Who? Did you tell your mom?"

"It was your grandma."

Phoebe's eyes went wide. "Oh my God. You told her?"

I shook my head. "She guessed."

"What? No way." Phoebe drew back, her expression somewhere between shock and outrage.

"She didn't know at the time," I clarified. "It wasn't until years later, probably around the time you came out, I guess. You'd been up for a visit, and I had made myself scarce while you were here, like I always did. After you left, Margery called me on it. She said she'd always wondered how you and I went from best friends to not speaking, and suddenly, it all made sense to her."

"Holy shit," Phoebe said. "I had no idea. Why didn't she ever ask me about it or tell me she knew?"

"I think she didn't want to overstep. She wanted you to tell her on your own."

"I never told anyone," Phoebe said quietly. "Not a single person, at least not until this week."

"I never did either."

"That's weird, isn't it?" She sat up, wrapping her arms around her knees. "I mean, you were so important to me. Our relationship was so foundational to me figuring out my identity. And *no one* knew."

"Well, your grandma did, and I think she would approve of what we're doing now. She always tried so hard to invite me over when you were in town," I told her.

Phoebe glanced at me. "You think she wanted us to be together?"

"Why wouldn't she? She adored you, and she and I were pretty close too."

"So, are we...you know, together?" she asked, still watching me intently.

"That's the question, isn't it?" I crossed one ankle over the other, turning my attention to the puffy clouds drifting overhead.

"And how do you want to answer it?"

"I don't know," I said honestly. Part of me wanted to jump in with both feet and make the most of every moment we had together before Phoebe left town, but my pragmatic side wanted to hit the brakes before we'd even gotten started. We'd had our night, and it had been amazing. Memories had been made, and the safe thing to do now was to pivot back to friendship before I got my heart broken by Phoebe a second time.

"You're doing a lot of thinking there," she said, narrowing her eyes at me.

"Then tell me what you're thinking," I deflected.

"Okay," she said with a nod. "My head says it's a terrible idea. I'm leaving town soon, and statistically, long-distance relationships have a high probability of failure. Not to mention, I just got out of a serious relationship, which means that again, statistically, you'd be my rebound, and those don't tend to work out either. If you look at the numbers, we're a terrible idea. But my heart tells a different story."

"What does your heart say?" I asked, almost terrified to hear the answer.

"My heart says we owe it to ourselves to see where this is going." She reached over and took my hand. "You're all I think about, Taylor. I thought I was going to spend my time in Vermont missing Sabrina and fuming about that meme, but I've barely thought about either since I got here. If I was truly heartbroken over losing her, I'd be miserable now. I wouldn't have gotten over her so easily."

"You sure seemed to get over me pretty easily last time," I said, knowing it was a cheap shot but unable to resist taking it.

"I didn't." Her voice trembled as she spoke. "I was an absolute mess that fall. I spent weeks crying in my bedroom. My parents were pulling out their hair trying to figure out what was wrong, but I was too terrified to tell them. I thought they'd disown me or throw me out of the house. That was overly dramatic thinking, but in my defense, I was sixteen."

I managed a smile. I didn't like hearing that she'd been as heartbroken as I was, but at least I could understand the feeling.

"Anyway, I felt terrible about running off on you, and I was so afraid you'd never speak to me again, even if I worked up the courage to call you. My mind was playing all kinds of tricks on me by then. Part of me hoped that if I just didn't think about you, I could go back to thinking I was straight. And the longer I waited to call you, the more convinced I became that you'd never be able to forgive me. I was a mess."

"I didn't know," I said.

"Of course you didn't, because I never called." Her gaze fell. "I'll forever be sorry about that."

"I could have called too, you know? Like you said, sixteen-year-olds aren't exactly known for their excellent decision-making skills."

"And that's what makes me want to try again," Phoebe said, raising her eyes to mine. "Don't we owe it to ourselves to give our relationship a real chance?"

"Jesus." I rubbed a hand over my face. "I don't know."

"Maybe we can get it right this time, Taylor."

"But you live in Boston," I reminded her.

"I do now, but that doesn't mean I have to live there forever."

"What are you saying?"

"I'm saying...let's not think about long-term logistics yet. Let's just make the most of our time together here in Vermont and see what happens."

"I don't want to start a relationship that doesn't have a chance of succeeding," I said, hearing the gruffness in my voice. "I'm a small-town girl at heart, Phoebe. I just want a simple life here with my family and my dogs. I'd be miserable if I tried to live in the city, and you love Boston. I couldn't ask you to give that up for me."

"Then don't ask," she whispered. "I don't know what the answer is—not yet anyway—but I know these hurdles aren't insurmountable. So I'm asking you for a fresh start. Let's just enjoy our time here together, and if we have something worth fighting for when it's time for me to leave, then let's fight for it."

I took a deep breath and blew it out. The logistics that Phoebe was so blasé about felt like a big deal to me. Her heart would always be in Boston, and I was powerless to change that. But at the same time, I was already too emotionally invested to *not* keep sleeping with her for however long she was in Vermont. "How about a compromise?" I suggested.

"Like what?" Phoebe asked, giving my fingers another squeeze.

"A summer fling," I said. "No regrets when it's time for you to leave."

"But we can reevaluate when the time comes?" she asked.

I shook my head. "Let's not make promises we can't keep. We're good at summer flings, right? Maybe that's all we're meant for."

"Taylor…" Her brows drew together.

"A summer fling," I insisted.

"Fine, if that's what you want to call it," she said. "But I'm not sixteen anymore. I'm not going to run off without a goodbye this time. And I'm not giving up on us without a fight either."

23

PHOEBE

"Hi," I said, not recognizing the soft, silly voice that came from my mouth.

Elizabeth the puppy squinted at me out of baby-blue eyes. She was the firstborn, the biggest, and now, the first puppy to open her eyes. I had definitely named her accurately, because she was a queen in the making. Right now, I held her on my knees, stroking her soft fur as I let her get her first good look at me.

"What do you think?" I asked the puppy. "How's life treating you so far?"

She blinked at me, looking bored at best. I was never quite sure what to say to them, but Taylor said it was important to get them used to the sound of my voice and that I should hold them regularly to get them used to that too.

At two weeks old, Elizabeth had almost doubled her birth weight, and now that her eyes were open, she looked so much more grown up. Suddenly, I could envision her—and the rest of the puppies—barreling around the house and getting into all kinds of trouble. For now, they only crawled around their playpen, but things would change soon, probably before I was ready for them to.

That seemed like a pretty good metaphor for my life right now, actually.

After spending a few minutes with Elizabeth, I weighed her and put her back in the pen, then repeated the process with the other three puppies. While I played with them, I texted back and forth with Courtney and Emily, the way we did most days since I'd been in Vermont and couldn't see them in person. I'd just finished weighing Cherry—who was still the smallest—when I heard Taylor knocking at the front door.

With a smile, I kissed the puppy on her little pink nose and set her back in the pen before rushing down the hall to greet Taylor. She'd come over after work every day this week, although she usually stopped at home first to drop off her dogs. It really would be easier if she could just bring them with her.

"Hey," I said as I opened the door, greeting her with a kiss.

"Hi." She stepped inside, bending to greet Violet, who'd joined us at the door, barking and wagging her tail. "Mm, it smells good in here."

"I put a roast in the crockpot this morning," I told her. "I've been hungry all day, smelling it while it cooked."

"I bet," she said. "How are the puppers?"

"Big. Oh, and Elizabeth's eyes opened."

"Aw." Taylor headed toward the bedroom to see for herself while I took the roast out of the crockpot.

It practically fell apart beneath my carving knife as I sliced it. I prepared two plates with beef, turnips, and potatoes and had just placed them on the table when Taylor came back down the hall.

"She's adorable with those little blue eyes," she said.

"Will they stay that blue?" I asked.

"Probably not," she said as she sat in the chair opposite mine. "They'll probably be brown like Violet's."

We dug into our food, falling silent for a few minutes while we ate.

"How do you feel about coming over to my place tomorrow night?" Taylor asked.

"Sure," I said. "Before V and V, you mean?" I wasn't performing this week, but she and I had made plans to go together anyway, like she did every Friday night.

She nodded. "I thought I could cook for us for a change before we go out, since Holly's going to stop by and check on Violet for you."

"I would feel bad about asking her to do that," I said, "but I've seen the way she looks at those puppies. She's totally smitten."

"Actually, it's more than that," Taylor said. "Remember how I told you about her senior dog who'd gotten too grumpy to let her foster anymore?"

I had a feeling this story was about to take a sad turn. "Yeah."

"Well, she found out last week that Candy has metastatic lung cancer."

"Oh no." My stomach swooped. I'd never met Holly's dog, but from the way she talked about her, I knew she loved Candy so much.

Taylor frowned at her plate. "It's the hardest part of pet ownership, you know? We're meant to outlive them, but that doesn't make it any easier. But between you and me, she's scoping out Violet's puppies for herself."

"She's going to adopt one?"

"She hasn't officially decided yet, but unofficially…yes."

"Oh, that makes me so happy," I said, then flinched. "I mean, not about Candy, obviously. But I'm glad one of the puppies will go home with her. They'll have the best life."

Taylor smiled as she cut a bite of her roast. "Yeah, I think it's going to work out perfectly. Hopefully a new puppy will help her through her grief."

"I hope so too. What about the other three? Has anyone applied to adopt them?"

"We've had a handful of applications, but nothing's official yet. I like to wait until the puppies are older and let people interact with them before we make a match."

"Makes sense," I told her. "And Holly should get first pick."

"She will," Taylor told me.

My phone chimed with an incoming text, and I glanced at it as I took another bite of the roast. Then I almost choked as I saw Sabrina's name gleaming on the screen. When I looked up, Taylor was staring at my phone.

"I didn't know you and Sabrina were still in touch," she said.

I swallowed my food and reached for my glass of water. My cheeks were hot, even though I hadn't done anything wrong. "We're not."

Taylor said nothing, turning her attention to her plate.

"She's texted me a few times since I got here, asking to talk," I explained. "I haven't responded."

"Maybe you should," Taylor said.

"I didn't know what to say, and I still don't."

"So you left town without a word?" Taylor said. "Sounds familiar."

"Whoa." I held my hands up. "No. She broke up with me, remember? She dumped me because she was upset about all the attention I was getting from that meme."

"Sorry," Taylor said. "That was uncalled for. Still, it seems like maybe you two should talk."

I clicked on Sabrina's text, revealing the words *I'm sorry* on the screen. "Maybe we should grab a coffee sometime when I'm back in Boston and have a civilized conversation for closure's sake, but it's over between us, Taylor."

"Are you sure?" she asked.

"Yes." Unlike my split from Taylor, this one was meant to be. To prove my point, I composed a quick text to Sabrina, telling her all the things I'd just told Taylor. "I'm glad she's realized she was an asshole for dumping me the way she did, but I've moved on."

Taylor gave me a hesitant smile. "Good for you."

I took her hand across the table. "So, your place tomorrow night?"

The following evening, I hopped in my car, headed for Taylor's apartment. I was curious to see it. So far, she'd always come to me, mostly because of Violet. I drove down Mountain Laurel Road and made a right. Ten minutes later, the big white colonial she'd told me to look for came into view. I spotted her SUV in the driveway where it wrapped around behind the house, and I pulled in behind her.

The house had a large yard with a swing set in back and various kids' toys scattered across the grass. I followed the walkway behind the house and descended three steps to the door to Taylor's basement apartment. I knocked and was greeted by Minnie's booming bark from inside. Moments later, her furry face appeared in the window, bouncing excitedly.

Taylor pulled the door open, waving me in. "Hi."

"Hey." I stepped into her arms and gave her a kiss, lingering there until Minnie's paws landed on my thigh. "Jealous much?" I asked the dog.

She barked, tail sweeping back and forth across the floor.

"I guess we're both excited to see you." Taylor hooked her hands into the back pockets of my jeans and grinned at me.

"Well, I'm excited to see you both too, one of you more than the other. No offense, Minnie."

"She's devastated," Taylor whispered as she tugged me closer.

"So I see." I brought my lips to hers as Minnie whined at my feet. We kissed, seemingly ravenous for each other, until I was gasping for breath and aching with need for her.

"Um," Taylor said when we came up for air, hazel eyes dancing with lust and amusement. "Do you want a tour, or should I take you straight to bed?"

"Funny." I nudged my forehead against hers. "Actually, I don't care about the tour right now."

"Good." She took my hand and tugged me through a door on the far side of the living room. I glimpsed wood-paneled walls and a row of small windows near the ceiling before she'd pushed me onto the bed. We scrambled out of our clothes in record time, and then Taylor settled herself against me, straddling my thigh as she bent her head to kiss me.

We'd been like this all week as we caught up on thirteen years of pent-up sexual tension. Often, sex was awkward the first few times with someone new, while we got to know each other's bodies, but that hadn't been the case with Taylor. We just dove in headfirst, and everything so far had been *great*.

She brought her hand between my thighs as she began to rock against me. My gasp mingled with her moan in the otherwise quiet bedroom. Taylor moved herself against my thigh while she stroked me with her fingers, and I basically just hung on for the ride, because *damn*, this was really working for me.

I came first, shuddering beneath her as release rushed through me. Taylor watched out of heavy-lidded eyes as she ground herself against my thigh, and then she was coming too. She threw her head back with a cry before lowering herself beside me on the bed. We lay together, panting and grinning like fools.

"So, welcome to my apartment," she said once she'd caught her breath. With one hand, she toyed with my hair, something she'd always done. I hadn't liked it when other girlfriends played with my hair, but something about Taylor's soft, soothing touch made me melt. Or maybe I hadn't liked it when other girlfriends played with my hair because it reminded me of Taylor, of our summer together.

"You have a great bed," I teased. "Not sure I can offer an opinion on anything else yet."

"We'd better fix that, then." She stood and took my hand, tugging me out of her bed.

We rinsed off together in a quick shower before we got dressed, and then I took the opportunity to explore her apartment while she popped a pizza in the oven for us. Her bedroom was a nice size, with a full-sized bed and a dresser against the back wall, which was made of white-painted cinder bricks beneath the windows overhead, making the room feel light and bright despite being mostly underground. The other three walls were wood paneled and covered in photos. I saw Taylor's parents, siblings, and grandparents, plus Minnie and numerous other dogs.

"How is your family?" I asked. I'd spent many afternoons with the Donovans as a girl, but I hadn't heard much about them over the years other than what my grandma had told me.

"Chaotic as ever," Taylor said, glancing affectionately at the wall of family photos. When I was younger, I'd been so jealous of Taylor's big, loving family. My parents were always fighting, always pitting me against each other, always making me feel guilty for escaping to Vermont during the summers. "Kelly is married now, with two kids," Taylor told me, pointing to a photo of her sister with her husband. "Both boys, and they're a handful, let me tell you."

"I bet." I sat on the edge of the bed as she walked from photo to photo, updating me on her family.

"Minnie adores them. She's so good with kids. Just look." Taylor picked up a photo that sat on the dresser, handing it to me. I saw two little boys with hair the same bright, cinnamon brown as their aunt. Minnie sat between them, tongue out and looking absolutely thrilled to have them hanging all over her.

"And Luke?" I asked, remembering Taylor's younger brother as a slightly geeky kid with braces who'd once put mud in our shoes while we were wading in the stream behind my grandma's house.

"He got married last summer," Taylor told me, pointing to another photo that showed a tall, handsome man I would never have recognized as that gawky kid, posing next to a beautiful blonde.

"Stop," I said with a giggle. "Little Luke is married?"

"He's twenty-seven now," she told me. "He doesn't give wedgies anymore or anything."

"Oh geez." I pressed a hand against my forehead. "Life goes on, doesn't it?"

"It sure does," she agreed. "My parents are pretty much the same, just older."

"Aw, I miss them," I said as she handed me another photo, showing an older couple I'd once known so well. They'd been almost like a second set of parents to me, a much warmer, happier version of my own. "Tell them hi for me, will you?"

She nodded. "I will."

We ate pizza together and then got in her SUV to drive into Burlington. V and V was bustling by the time we got there, nearly every bar stool taken and a man with a guitar on the stage in back, singing an acoustic version of Aerosmith's "Walk this Way." As much as I enjoyed performing, tonight I couldn't wait to sit back and enjoy someone else's music.

"Oh look, there are Brendan and Elsie," Taylor said, gesturing toward one of the tables in the middle of the room.

"Friends of yours?" I asked.

She nodded. "Mind if we say hello?"

"I'm the social butterfly between us, remember?" I said, nudging her forward. "I'd love to meet your friends."

We crossed the room, and Taylor introduced me to Brendan and Elsie, who seemed thrilled that she'd brought a date to the bar tonight. We dragged over two chairs to join them and spent the next several hours drinking cider and sharing lively conversation. It was one of the best nights I'd had since arriving in Vermont. There were few things I loved more than a night out on the town with friends, and to do it with Taylor made it that much more special.

As we left later that evening, I hooked my arm through Taylor's. "I had so much fun tonight."

"Me too," she said, giving me an easy smile.

"We should do it again." This was the first time we'd ever hung out together as a couple in a social setting, and I liked it so much.

"Actually," she said as she clicked the lock on her SUV. Its lights flashed, and we each climbed into our respective seats. "My cousin Steven is getting married in a few weeks, and I still need a date. My whole family will be there, and I know they'd love to see you. Want to come with me?"

"As your date?" My breath caught in my throat.

"Or as my friend," she said as she started the car. "It's just a casual wedding at one of the county parks. We'll have a barbeque and dancing in the picnic shelter."

"This feels like a big deal." I pressed a hand against my chest. Sure, Taylor's family had always liked me, but they knew me as her friend, not her lover. To attend her cousin's wedding as her date made our relationship feel real in a way it hadn't before.

"It's just a casual thing," she said, lips pinched as if she was already regretting her invitation. "A chance for you to catch up with my family."

But whether she realized it yet or not, this would be a turning point in our relationship. She could pretend this was just a summer fling, but if I went to the wedding, I would be giving our relationship permanence by letting her family know it existed. I couldn't go back to Boston this time and pretend it never happened, nor did I want to. Her family would want updates. They'd want to know what happened if I left town.

I took her hand. "I would *love* to go as your wedding date."

24

TAYLOR

Looking back, I should have seen a bump coming, because our first two weeks together had just been *too* easy. When my phone rang in the dark hours of the night, fear gripped my stomach before I'd even opened my eyes. No good news ever came at this hour. I fumbled for my phone, dislodging Minnie from where she lay pressed against me. Phoebe's name gleamed on my screen.

"Phoebe?" I mumbled as I connected the call, my voice rough and scratchy from sleep. "Everything okay?"

"No," she said, and her voice sounded too loud in my ear, almost like she was shouting. "Something's wrong with Cherry. She's listless and cold. I already called Dr. Thompson and left a message, but I don't know what to do."

I blew out a breath. This was bad, but it was nothing I hadn't dealt with before. Foster pets had medical emergencies all the time, especially since they often came into the shelter from less-than-ideal situations. We did everything we could for every single one of them, and I grieved when one passed away, but I tried to keep an emotional distance, since they weren't mine. If I got my heart broken every time one died, eventually it would drain my spirit.

"I've got Dr. Thompson's home number," I told Phoebe. "I'll

give her a call, and she'll probably be able to meet us at her office, but if not, she'll give me the number of the local vet who's covering for her tonight. There are a few. In the meantime, I need you to get dressed and get that portable heating pad I gave you, the one that heats up in the microwave. Warm it up for Cherry, and then you can put her in a box with the heating pad for the ride to the vet. I'll meet you there."

"Okay," she whispered, but I heard her voice tremble. She'd had a soft spot for Cherry ever since her dramatic entrance into the world, and this might be the first time Phoebe had dealt with a pet's medical emergency. It could be terrifying. I knew that well. "Thanks for coming with me," she said.

"Of course." I told her. I could have just given her the vet's info and asked her to call me with an update. That's what I would have done for any of my other foster homes, but this was Phoebe, and she was important to me. Not to mention, she was an inexperienced first-time foster parent who I'd pushed into taking on a challenging case. "I'm going to hang up now so I can make those calls. You start getting ready, and I'll call you right back."

"Thank you," she said. "Bye."

I ended the call and dialed Dr. Thompson at home. It rang long enough that I thought it was going to go to voicemail, and then she picked up, sounding sleepy but alert. "Hello?"

"Hi, Dr. Thompson. It's Taylor Donovan. Sorry to wake you, but I have an emergency with one of Violet's puppies."

"What's wrong?" she asked, now sounding wide awake.

"Phoebe says she's listless and cold. It's Cherry, the littlest puppy, the one who wasn't breathing when she was born."

"Right." I could hear her jotting something down. "Her heart and lungs sounded good at her exam, but there may be something going on internally that I wasn't aware of. Can you have Phoebe meet me at the clinic in thirty minutes?"

"Yes. Thank you so much. I'll be there too."

"I'll see you then." With a click, she was gone.

I scrambled out of bed, and Minnie moved in to take my spot, resting her fluffy face on my pillow while she watched me get dressed. In the corner, Blue watched from inside his crate. I threw on jeans and a T-shirt while I called Phoebe to update her, and then I went into the bathroom. Five minutes later, I was in my car, headed for the clinic.

My headlights sliced through the night as I finally thought to glance at the clock. It was almost three in the morning. I navigated the winding roads easily in the dark, having lived here my whole life, but a little part of me was worried about Phoebe doing the same. Maybe I should have offered to pick her up.

I caught movement out of the corner of my eye a moment before a deer leaped in front of my car. Instinctively, my foot was on the brake almost before I'd realized what was happening. The seat belt caught, keeping me upright as the tires squealed and the car swung. My stomach swooped while shock prickled through my system.

The car screeched to a stop, headlights blazing into the dense trees in front of me. I gripped the steering wheel, gasping for breath while I gathered my wits. I was okay. I hadn't hit the deer. There had been no impact. I was sure about that part. I'd spun the car ninety degrees and was now sitting broadside across the road.

I backed up and straightened out the car before someone came along and hit me, pulling to the side of the road for a minute to recover. I forced myself to take slow, deep breaths until my heart rate slowed and my hands stopped shaking so badly. Then I pulled back onto the road, because Phoebe was waiting for me at the clinic.

I drove more slowly this time as my eyes darted from one side of the road to the other, wary of every shadow. Fifteen minutes later, I pulled into the vet's parking lot. A single streetlamp illuminated the small lot in its yellowish glow, revealing Phoebe's purple Nissan.

I shut off the engine and climbed out of my SUV, crossing quickly to her car. I slid into the passenger seat, lifting the small box there into my lap. Cherry was inside, snuggled in a blanket and not moving.

"Thanks for coming," Phoebe said in a hushed voice.

"Of course." I reached over to rest my hand on hers as I looked down at the puppy. "She really doesn't look good, does she?"

"It happened so fast," Phoebe said. "I mean, her growth has always been the slowest, but she's been on a steady curve."

"She may have had something going on inside her since she was born that we didn't know about, and it's just manifested to the point that it's causing outward symptoms. That happens a lot in young puppies, when their bodies are growing so fast."

"Will she be okay?" Phoebe asked.

"I have no idea," I told her honestly. "But if she's not, please don't blame yourself. You've done everything for her that you possibly could."

Phoebe blew out a breath. "That's not very reassuring."

"She might be perfectly fine," I told her. "But when things go wrong in tiny puppies, sometimes there's nothing we can do. Hopefully we'll know more in a few minutes."

Headlights illuminated the parking lot behind us, and Dr. Thompson's SUV turned into the lot. Seconds later, she was motioning us toward the front door as she unlocked it for us.

Phoebe stood from the car and leaned over to take the box from my lap. "Thank you so much for coming out in the middle of the night," she said to the vet.

"It's part of the job," Dr. Thompson said. "And I'm happy to do it."

We followed her into the clinic and directly into the exam room. She flipped on lights as she walked, and we all blinked against the sudden fluorescent glow.

"This is the runt, correct?" she asked as she took the box from Phoebe's hands.

She nodded. "Cherry Parfait."

"Right." Dr. Thompson's lips twitched with a smile as she lifted the puppy out of the box. "Our littlest rose."

Phoebe and I watched as she examined the puppy, who let out a high-pitched squeal as she was removed from her cozy nest. Cherry's little feet waved in the air as Dr. Thompson listened to her heart and lungs. She looked at Cherry's eyes and ears, listened to her heart and lungs, and then gently prodded her abdomen, prompting another squeal.

"Well," she said as she tucked Cherry back into her box, nestled against the heating pad. "I'm feeling some enlargement in her liver."

"Oh no," Phoebe gasped, gripping the edge of the exam room table.

"I'd like to run some bloodwork, and depending on the results, I'm probably going to refer you to the veterinary hospital in Burlington."

Phoebe nodded, her eyes wide. "Is that bad? Enlargement in her liver? It sounds bad."

"Anything is potentially serious when we're talking about a puppy this young," the vet told her. "But it could be benign and treatable. We'll know more once we've run some tests. I'm going to take her in back for a minute to draw some blood." She lifted the box and left through the door at the other side of the exam room.

Phoebe turned toward me, and I wrapped her in my arms. She pressed her face against my shoulder, and I rubbed a hand up and down her back.

"It's going to be okay," I told her.

"She's so little. Fostering is hard," she murmured against my shirt. "I didn't expect to get this emotionally attached."

"Occupational hazard of the foster mom," I said.

Dr. Thompson returned a few minutes later with Cherry in her box. "I'll send her bloodwork to be processed as soon as the lab opens. In the meantime, I gave her some extra fluids. The hospital in Burlington will be expecting your call once they open at eight."

"So I just take her home for now?" Phoebe asked.

The vet nodded. "She's best off resting at home with Violet and her siblings until her appointment at the hospital."

We thanked her for her help and walked outside into the dimly lit parking lot. Around us, the woods were dark and quiet. I tucked Cherry's box into Phoebe's car and turned to her. "If you need anything, I'm only a phone call away."

25

PHOEBE

I sat alone in the exam room of the ironically named Cherry Street Veterinary Clinic in Burlington later that morning, waiting for Cherry and wishing Taylor were here with me. She was at work, although she'd told me she could probably leave early if I needed her.

I needed her, all right, and not just because Cherry was sick. Lately, I couldn't seem to get enough of Taylor. The cabin was almost ready to rent, but I wasn't ready to leave. I wanted to see things through for Violet and the puppies if I could. I'd done several financial consultations for local businesses over the last few weeks, and it had given me enough spending money to stay...for now.

Cherry's bloodwork had indeed shown elevated liver enzymes, and now she was somewhere in back, undergoing an ultrasound to see what was going on with her liver. This was all so much more than I'd signed up for when I came to Vermont. I'd only wanted a place to hide for a little while, and here I was a month later, completely smitten with Taylor and awaiting medical news on a tiny foster puppy whose wellbeing had become unexpectedly important to me.

The door to the exam room opened, and the vet entered. He

was a few years older than me, with blond hair and a friendly smile.

"Emmett Moore," he said, extending a hand.

I stood and took it. "Phoebe Shaw."

"Your foster puppy has had quite a rough day." His expression was empathetic, which I appreciated, but the fact that Cherry wasn't with him seemed like bad news.

"Is she all right?" I asked.

"The ultrasound showed a large mass on her liver," he told me, and my stomach dipped. "I'd like to get her in for emergency surgery to remove it."

"Oh, wow." I swallowed. "Is it cancer?"

"We won't know that until we biopsy the mass after it's removed, but in a puppy her age, it's probably benign. We see these types of tumors develop sometimes. It may have been growing undetected since birth, given the difficulties she's had."

"So you can do surgery on a puppy that little?" I asked, hoping it wasn't a stupid question.

"Yes, we can. I know it's hard to think about, but she's in good hands, I promise."

"Thanks," I told him.

"When you bring a puppy named Cherry into the Cherry Street Veterinary Clinic, you know she's going to get the star treatment." He rested a hand briefly on my shoulder, and I smiled, grateful to him for putting me at ease. "Do you need me to talk to someone from the shelter to get authorization?"

Right. This was probably going to be expensive, and Cherry wasn't mine. "I'll call. You'd do the surgery today, if they approve it?"

Dr. Moore nodded. "I've got an opening this afternoon, and I'd like to get her right in if possible."

"Okay. Is it all right if I sit in here to call the shelter and get authorization?"

"Sure thing," he told me. "I'll check back in a few minutes."

I pulled my cell phone out of my purse and dialed Taylor.

"Hi," she said when the line connected. "Any news on Cherry?"

"Yeah. She has a tumor growing on her liver, and they want to do emergency surgery right away."

"Damn," Taylor breathed. "Any idea what kind of prognosis they're giving her?"

"He said they wouldn't know much until they remove it, but since it seems to be growing pretty rapidly, it needs to come out whether it's cancerous or not."

"All right." The clattering of a keyboard echoed over the line. "Our funds are—as always—low, but I'll organize a fundraiser for Cherry. The community usually comes through for us when something like this happens. I can't imagine that they won't come through for an precious little puppy like Cherry. Just remind Emmett to give us our usual discount? And we'll need a payment plan. I can authorize you to charge two hundred to the rescue's card today for a down payment."

"I'll tell him. Thanks, Taylor."

I ended the call as the vet came back into the exam room. We worked out the payment details, and then I was in my car, headed home without Cherry. When I got there, I went straight to the bedroom to check on Violet and the other puppies. She seemed calm, not overly concerned about her missing baby, which was a little bit surprising, but maybe she was able to live in the moment in a way most people weren't.

The idea of freedom from the mistakes of my past or worry about the future felt awfully enticing. And in fact, maybe it was what I should be focusing on. Maybe I should be savoring every moment with Taylor instead of worrying what our future held. As I watched Violet grooming her three healthy puppies, I vowed to try harder to live in the present.

I'd planned to go shopping for accents and artwork for the main living areas today, but I was too tired after having been up half the night with Cherry. Instead, I climbed into bed and dozed off. The sound of my phone ringing yanked me back to consciousness. I blinked as I rolled over, looking for my phone. It was on the table by the bed, and my dad's name flashed on the screen. I connected the call. "Hey, Dad."

"Hi, sweetie. Are you okay? You sound a little hoarse."

"Oh, sorry. I was asleep," I told him, clearing my throat to rid myself of my sleep voice. "I was up most of the night with a puppy medical emergency, so I just took a nap."

"That's not good. I'm sorry I woke you," he said.

"It's fine. What's up?"

"How's the puppy?" he asked.

"She's having emergency surgery this afternoon to remove a mass from her liver. Hopefully, I'll hear something soon."

"That sounds serious." He paused. "And also expensive."

"The shelter pays for all of it," I told him.

"Well, that's good."

"Yeah." I snuggled further under the quilt.

"Anyway, I was calling to let you know that I've decided not to sell the cabin," he told me, and even though it was the news I'd expected, my stomach still sank knowing Taylor wouldn't get her wish.

"Okay, well, thanks for at least thinking about it," I said. My phone beeped, indicating I had another call. "Dad? I need to go. I think the vet's calling with an update about the puppy."

"All right, dear. I'll talk to you later."

"Bye," I told him, then connected the call. "Hello?"

"Is this Phoebe Shaw?" a male voice asked.

"Yes, this is Phoebe."

"Hi, Phoebe, this is Emmett Moore from the Cherry Street Veterinary Clinic. I'm calling to let you know that Cherry came through surgery well. We successfully removed the mass on her liver and sent it off to be biopsied at the state lab."

"Oh good," I breathed. "How is she?"

"She's just starting to come out from under the anesthesia. Given her age and size, she'll need to stay overnight at the least," he told me.

I cringed because that sounded expensive, but I was also glad she'd have medical professionals watching over her for the time being instead of me. "Is it okay for her to be away from her mom like that?"

"Oh, sure," he said. "She's resting comfortably in an incubator for warmth. If she's alert enough, we'll bottle feed her tonight, but we can tube feed if necessary."

"Tube feed?" My voice rose.

"It's not as scary as it sounds. We just put a small flexible tube down her throat into her stomach to deliver formula to her that way if she's unable to drink on her own."

Well, that didn't exactly put a comforting image in my mind, but I supposed that as long as she got the nourishment she needed, that was the important thing. "And will she be able to nurse again once she's back home?"

"In all likelihood, yes," he said. "There's no medical reason why she couldn't, but occasionally, a puppy might develop a preference for a bottle, or her mother might reject her once she's been separated."

"Oh." I glanced over at Violet, who was currently grooming Sunny. She was a great mama, but she had briefly rejected Cherry when she was born not breathing.

"She'll probably resume nursing like a champ," he said. "And if not, you'll only have to bottle feed her for a few weeks before she's old enough to wean."

"Assuming she's okay," I said, voicing my lingering fear.

"That's right," he agreed, sounding more somber now. "If the tumor is malignant, I'll be honest with you, her prognosis is not good. However, there's every reason to believe it was benign, in which case, I'm hopeful she'll make a full recovery."

As it turned out, Cherry spent two days in the hospital. While she was away, I spent most of my free time working on financial consultations for local businesses. I hadn't been sure if anyone would respond to my Facebook postings, but my grandma had been a popular lady around here, and now it seemed like everyone who had known her wanted me to come in and give them financial advice.

I set up my laptop at the kitchen table, where I could work without the constant squealing and squawking of puppies. They were three weeks old now and starting to wobble around the playpen on their own, which was absolutely adorable. Violet didn't stay with them all the time anymore. Sometimes, she'd come down the hall and lie on the dog bed in the living room near me for a little break. I trusted her judgment on that, and so far, everything seemed to be fine.

I spent the afternoon finishing up some numbers for Mrs. Ashton's yarn shop, and then it was time to pick up Cherry from the vet. The hospital was about forty minutes away, and I spent the whole drive worrying over her prognosis and the care she would require once she was home, envisioning tiny stitches and bandages. I wasn't very good with wounds. I never had been. Just the thought made me shudder.

When I arrived, a vet tech took me back to an empty exam room, and a few minutes later, Dr. Moore entered.

"Hi there," he said. "You'll be relieved to know that Cherry's biopsy came up negative."

"Oh," I said, feeling a welcome rush of relief. "That's great news."

He nodded. "Her bloodwork so far indicates that her liver is functioning normally, so we're cautiously optimistic that there won't be any issues. We'll need to see her again in a few days for a recheck."

He spent the next ten minutes or so going over all her care with me, and by the time he went to get Cherry, my head was spinning. He carried her in the same box I'd brought her here in two days ago, except she was lying on her side now, revealing a row of silver staples along her belly that made me vaguely nauseous.

Consequently, I was already reaching for my phone as I walked to the parking lot with her. "Can you stay with me tonight?" I asked when Taylor connected the call. "I'm so worried about caring for Cherry and keeping her incision safe, and...I don't have any experience with anything like this."

"Yeah, let me just find someone to watch Minnie for me, but I should be able to do that, no problem," she said.

"What about Blue?"

"He was adopted this morning." I could hear the smile in Taylor's voice.

"Aw, good for him."

"Yep," Taylor said. "He went home with a woman who lives alone and was looking for a loyal companion. I think they'll be a perfect match."

"That does sound perfect for him," I agreed, still boggled by how she could care for a dog and then give it up. I was already attached to Violet and her puppies, torn between wondering how I was going to say goodbye and wishing they were already gone so I could finish up with the cabin and get back to Boston...unless I found a way to stay here with Taylor.

"So how is Cherry?" she asked.

"Well, her biopsy came up negative, which is the good news. As long as her liver keeps working and nothing else goes wrong, she should be okay." I tucked her box into the passenger seat and wrapped the seat belt around it to keep it in place. Cherry stared up at me out of squinty, baby-blue eyes. "I'm just worried about her recovery right now."

"I'll come over in an hour or so, all right? Don't panic in the meantime. She'll be fine. The littlest ones tend to be the quickest to heal, you know?"

"If you say so. And thank you."

I ended the call and drove home carefully, sneaking glances at Cherry the whole time. She fell asleep a few minutes into the drive and slept the rest of the way home. When I got there, I carried her inside, and, as Dr. Moore had suggested, I held the box out to let Violet sniff her when she greeted me at the front door. Violet gave her several enthusiastic licks—which seemed like a good sign—before sniffing at her belly.

"I have to put this silly little sock shirt on her before I can give her back to you," I told Violet. One of the vet techs had cut head and leg holes through a couple of old socks for Cherry to wear to protect her incision from her siblings' paws and Violet's grooming attempts. Even so, I was going to have to keep a close eye on her...and she might not be able to go back in with her littermates at all. It was going to be a process of trial and error to see how they all reacted.

Violet followed on my heels as I walked to the bedroom. I set Cherry's box on the bed and opened the bag of supplies the hospital had sent home with me, pulling out one of the sock shirts. She whimpered as I lifted her from the box. Trying my hardest not to look at her incision, I worked her wiggly legs through the openings on the sock and slid it down her body. It was harder than I'd expected due to her constant squirming. Her legs never seemed to be where I needed them.

But finally, I had it. The sock actually had little cherries on it, and oh my *God*, it was possibly the cutest thing I'd ever seen. I set her on the bedspread and took some pictures with my phone that Taylor could post on the shelter's blog for their fundraiser. Cherry watched me for a minute in confusion, then scrunched up her eyes and howled for her mama.

"Okay, okay," I told her. I pressed a kiss against her forehead and then set her in the playpen. My chest felt suddenly heavy as I watched her crawl across the bedding toward her siblings. Would they take her back? What if they ripped out one of her staples, regardless of the shirt?

Violet climbed in and lay down, sniffing at Cherry. She nuzzled the shirt, attempting to get her nose beneath it, probably wanting to lick Cherry's incision.

"Violet, no," I told her.

She looked up at me with those soulful eyes before returning her attention to her puppy. Cherry settled in to nurse, only to be toppled by Elizabeth. The puppy rolled belly up, squealing loudly, and my heart catapulted into my throat. Had she popped a staple? Had she done internal damage? What was I thinking even trying to put her back in with her siblings?

I scooped her up and brought her with me to the bed, where I lay on my back and settled her on my chest. She crawled over to lie in the crook of my arm and closed her eyes. I hadn't seen any blood on the shirt, so I was going to assume the incision was okay for now.

With Cherry's warm, solid weight resting against my heart, I tried to relax, hoping Taylor got here soon, because I had absolutely no idea what I was doing. I should have checked when Cherry had been fed last before I lay down, but since she seemed content, I wasn't going to disturb her until Taylor got here.

Luckily, I didn't have to wait long. Taylor knocked at the front door about ten minutes later, and I called out to her, hoping I wouldn't have to move Cherry. "Come on in."

The door creaked open, and then I heard Taylor's footsteps in the hall. She entered the bedroom, wearing her usual jeans and T-shirt, her hair pulled back in a ponytail. A dreamy smile passed over her face as she saw me lying in bed with Cherry. "How's it going?"

"I'm scared to put her back in with her siblings, in case they mess with her staples. Elizabeth knocked her over the minute I set her down."

"What did the vet say?" Taylor sat on the bed beside me, rubbing Cherry's head as I went over everything Dr. Moore had told me. As she listened, she gently rolled Cherry onto her side and lifted the shirt to inspect the incision. I averted my eyes. Just the sight of those staples in her skin made my stomach squirm. "Don't worry," Taylor told me. "We've got this. I haven't cared for a puppy this tiny post-op before, but I've cared for plenty of larger ones."

"I'm so glad you're here," I told her, leaning over to give her a kiss.

"And I can stay a couple of nights if you need me," she said. "Minnie's with my sister."

"Oh my God." Everything inside me seemed to loosen and get lighter. Not only would I have help with Cherry, but I'd get to spend several nights with Taylor. What had felt like a scary and burdensome ordeal suddenly seemed almost fun. "That's too good to be true, Taylor. Really?"

She grinned at me. "Really."

26

TAYLOR

I sat cross legged in the middle of the bed with Cherry positioned across my knees as I brought the bottle to her mouth. I hadn't bottle-fed a puppy before, but I had cared for a litter of abandoned kittens once, so I figured it would be similar. The veterinary hospital had sent a packet of detailed instructions home with Phoebe, so I wasn't worried. Cherry took the bottle easily, eyes closing as she began to suck down her formula.

"You can tell she's had a few days' practice at this while she was in the hospital," I said, hoping to reassure Phoebe, who was clearly fearful about caring for a post-op puppy.

Phoebe leaned forward to watch. "You make that look easy."

"Cherry's doing all the work," I said. We'd tried putting her back in with her siblings, but she'd gotten knocked around a lot, and Violet kept trying to remove her shirt, so we'd decided to bottle-feed her for now. Hopefully, in a few days, when she was stronger and the incision wasn't so fresh, we'd be able to get her nursing again.

The puppy made cute little slurping noises as she ate. I held the bottle steady, tipping it just enough to help her drink without overwhelming her with milk. I'd been able to mix her medication into the formula, so we were killing two birds with one stone here. "This sock shirt with the cherries on it is the cutest fucking thing. Did you make that for her?" I asked.

"No," Phoebe told me. "Someone at the hospital did."

After Cherry finished her bottle, I cleaned her up, since I couldn't let Violet do the job at the moment. Then I tucked the puppy into her box with the portable heating pad to keep her cozy while she napped. I snuggled closer to Phoebe on the bed, and she wrapped an arm around me, drawing me close.

Lying here with her in the master bedroom of Margery's cabin, everything felt upside down. I'd hoped this bedroom would be mine, that this cabin would be mine. I'd hoped I'd never see Phoebe again, and then I'd hoped she would leave town before I was foolish enough to fall for her again. And yet, here we were.

"This isn't what I thought Vermont was going to look like," Phoebe murmured, one hand splayed across my stomach beneath my shirt. "I thought I'd fix up this cabin and be on my way back to Boston by now."

"Any progress on that front?" I asked, determined not to let her know how much I wished she could stay.

She shook her head. "I had a Skype interview last week, but I haven't heard anything more about it."

"Have you applied for many jobs?" I felt somewhat guilty that I hadn't been more supportive of her job hunt so far. She owned a condo in Boston. Her friends and family were there. It was where she lived, and nothing I said or did would change that.

"Yeah," she said. "Everything I can find. I need a real paycheck."

"How is your consulting going?"

"Pretty good. It's enough to tide me over until I find a permanent job."

"Could it be more than that?" I asked, hardly daring to hope.

"Enough to live on?" she asked. "No, and I think soon I'll have run through all of my grandma's friends who needed their finances checked. I need a real job."

"Yes," I agreed.

"My dad called the other day," she said quietly.

"Oh?"

"He still doesn't want to sell. I'm sorry, Taylor."

"It's okay," I said automatically, even though it wasn't. I'd let myself get my hopes up that Phoebe would be able to give me at least one of the things I wanted, and if I couldn't have *her*, this cabin was the next best thing. Now, for the first time, I truly grasped that I was going to lose it too. I was going to have to watch tourists tromp around on this land that should have been mine, and I was going to hate every moment of it.

"For what it's worth, I really wanted you to have it," she said.

"I appreciate that." I rolled toward her, burying my face in the soft fabric of her shirt. At least now I knew, and I could start preparing myself for the inevitable.

"Cherry looks comfy over there," Phoebe said as her fingers drifted slowly back and forth across my back. "I was afraid she'd be crying in pain or look really sick...I don't really know what I expected, but right now, she looks like a healthy sleeping puppy in silly clothes."

"Puppies are so resilient," I said. "She'll bounce back in no time." And hopefully, so would I.

"Are you hungry?" she asked.

"Yeah." I nuzzled my face against her neck. "And I have everything I need right here."

"Do you?" She gasped as I slid my tongue along the underside of her jaw. Her skin was so sensitive there, and I never tired of tasting her.

"I sure do." I gripped her bare thigh as I placed hot, open-mouthed kisses across her throat and over her chest. I'd never thought bone structure could be beautiful until I'd fallen for Phoebe, but there was something so...elegant about the curve of her collarbones. She was built like a dancer, small and petite, and yet, she had no rhythm.

She wasn't particularly athletic either. I was often the one encouraging her to hike farther, to explore the next hill or curve in the path, when she would have been content to stick her feet in the stream and daydream in the sunshine. Without her, I never remembered to take those breaks. I'd shown her the top of the mountain, and she'd shown me the way it felt to close my eyes and feel the whisper of the breeze against my cheeks.

And right now, I wanted to show her stars. I teased the hem of her shorts with my fingers while I explored her collarbones with my tongue. Phoebe's breath hitched as she exhaled. The warm, sweet scent of her lotion seemed infused with her skin, like she was literally a treat waiting to be eaten.

My fingers slid beneath the hem of her shorts, exploring the soft skin below. Maybe it was our teenage make-out sessions that had given me such a fixation with these parts of her body. She hadn't been ready for me to take off her clothes back then, so I'd spent hours worshipping every exposed inch of her skin, and now I fell back into old habits, exploring the valley between her breasts and the strip of stomach visible above her shorts where her top had ridden up.

But Phoebe wasn't as patient as she used to be. She grabbed my wandering hand and brought it to the button on her shorts, a not-so-subtle invitation. I popped the button as she reached for my jeans, making me suddenly aware of the need burning inside me. She dragged down my zipper, and her fingers continued on their journey, rubbing against me right where I ached for her.

"Phoebe," I whispered.

"Yes?" she asked, her face all wide-eyed innocence while her fingers continued to tease me over my jeans.

I love you. The words almost spilled from my lips before I could stop them, but the realization hardly came as a surprise. Some part of me had been in love with her since we were kids, and a part of me probably always would be. "You're killing me here," I murmured as I arched into her touch.

"In a good way, I hope." She pushed at the waistband of my jeans, and I wiggled out of them.

"Always." I helped her out of her shorts, crawling down to

trace the edge of her underwear with my tongue. Her panties were a deep green, the color of the forest canopy outside. I already knew what I'd find when I removed her tank top, but when I bared the matching bra, my pulse jumped at the discovery that there was a small pink rose embroidered between her breasts. "Sexy," I whispered before giving it a gentle tug with my teeth.

Phoebe sat up, mahogany curls hanging over her shoulders and the prettiest blush darkening her cheeks as she yanked at my T-shirt. I lifted it over my head, and then we were both in our underwear. I sat there for a moment, just taking in the sight of her before me in her sexy green lingerie.

A puppy squealed, and we both turned automatically to check on Cherry, but she was fast asleep in her box. Blaze was trying to climb over Sunny in the whelping pen, and Sunny wasn't happy about it. Violet watched idly, letting them work it out on their own.

"The guest room," Phoebe said, sliding off the bed, and I followed her across the hall.

We stripped each other out of our underwear and sank onto the twin bed together. It might be smaller than the one we'd just left, but this bed had seen every stage of our relationship. Phoebe straddled my lap, pushing me flat against the bedspread. She leaned forward, bringing our lips together as she began to rock against me.

I could feel her wetness against my skin, and it fueled my own desire. We rolled onto our sides, threading our legs so we could both get the friction we needed. We moved against each other, hands roaming everywhere. I played with her nipples until they'd tightened into hard buds, then bent my head to take one in my mouth while my fingers circled her clit as she ground herself against my thigh.

"Yes," she breathed, moving faster. Her fingernails bit into my back, drawing me closer against her, and her thigh shifted between mine, somehow sending me right over the edge.

I moaned, hips bucking as my orgasm washed through me. I

kept stroking Phoebe, kept kissing her until she'd joined me, jerking in my arms as she found release. Afterward, we lay together in a tangle of arms and legs and several curly strands of her hair.

"I'm so glad you're staying here for a few days," she murmured. "Not only to have your help with Cherry, but just to have this time with you. It's going to be so great."

"Yeah," I said, my voice gone a little bit gruff. I was looking forward to it too, but I also knew it was going to make it harder to give her up…and the cabin too.

"And in all seriousness, are you hungry?" she asked with a naughty smile. "Because I'm starving. I need to go shopping, but I could throw together some pasta or something. My last few days got totally sidetracked by Cherry."

"Pasta sounds good to me. One of us can go shopping tomorrow."

"That's the handy thing about having someone else here with me," she said as she sat up, tucking her hair behind her ears. "I don't know what I would have done here by myself. I'm so scared to leave her. I'm already worried that we left her in the other room."

Warmth spread through my chest as it always did when Phoebe went soft for her foster pups. "Then let's go check on her."

27

PHOEBE

Taylor and I sat with our feet in the stream, letting the icy water wash over our toes for as long as either of us could stand it. Although it was mid-June now, the water flowing down from the Green Mountains was still cold. We'd brought the Adirondack chairs from my grandma's patio down to the stream because there was just no better sound in the world, as far as I was concerned. It splashed and babbled past us, crystal clear and moving fast.

Cherry was snuggled in a blanket-lined laundry basket beside me, wearing a baby-blue shirt. She'd been home almost a week and was recovering well. Every day, she was visibly stronger, and this morning she'd successfully nursed with her siblings for the first time. Violet lay next to the laundry basket, watching over her baby. She'd been surprisingly mellow about all of this, seemingly unfazed by Cherry's illness and the changes her recovery had brought.

"I could get used to this," I said as I wiggled my toes under the water, watching the way my pink nail polish rippled beneath the surface.

"Don't get *too* used to it," Taylor said, darting a glance in my direction. She did that every time I hinted that I wanted to stay, and I wasn't sure what to make of it. Did she want me to leave, or

176

was she holding me at arms' length to keep herself from getting hurt?

I didn't want to hurt her. I hadn't then, and I definitely didn't now. I didn't necessarily want to leave either. As much as I missed my friends and my condo in Boston, I knew I would miss Taylor even more when and if I went home to stay.

"Getting cold feet already," I joked as I pulled my feet out of the stream. I dried them off and tucked them beneath me in my chair to warm up. "Seriously, though. I'm doing a lot of financial consults. I should be able to stay until these guys are weaned."

"That's good," Taylor said, swiping her foot back and forth through the running water. She had more tolerance for the cold than I did. "Soon they'll be running all over your house, though, so be forewarned."

"Yeah, I noticed."

They were starting to romp and play inside their pen, and Taylor had started bringing them outside after they ate to see if they'd use the bathroom on their own. We'd had to line their pen with absorbent pads now that they were starting to pee independently.

"I'm not thrilled about them peeing on my brand-new floors, but we just won't include that part in the rental listing," I said.

"As long as you can get the smell out."

"I'm going to cover the entire kitchen in pee pads and keep them in there," I told her, only half joking.

Violet got to her feet and walked to the edge of the stream, dipping her head for a drink. She slurped noisily before shoving her dripping face into the laundry basket to sniff Cherry. The puppy yipped, reaching toward her.

"You want some one-on-one bonding time?" I picked up the puppy and handed her to Taylor while I spread the blanket from inside the basket over the grass.

Taylor leaned over to set the puppy on the blanket. She toddled across it in her little blue shirt, and Violet settled in beside her, tail wagging. Cherry stumbled over her mom's outstretched paws and nipped at her tail before settling in for a snack. Her ears twitched back and forth while she nursed.

"Steven's wedding is this weekend, right?" I asked, because Taylor hadn't mentioned it in a while, and I was wondering if she had changed her mind about bringing me.

She nodded, watching Cherry and Violet. "Still want to come?"

"I do, as long as you're okay with introducing me to your family as your date."

She looked at me then, and I felt the same hesitance from her that I'd been sensing more often lately. "I don't have to introduce you as my date. We could attend as friends."

"Well, I want to be your date," I told her. "I'm ready for people to know that you're not just my friend, Taylor."

"It feels like a moot point when you're about to leave town." She stuck her feet back in the water.

"I'm not in a hurry to leave," I told her.

"What's that supposed to mean?" she asked.

"It means I'm trying to stay as long as I can. I'd like to see where this thing between us is going. Stop acting like I've got one foot out the door."

"But you do," she insisted. "Phoebe, if I show you around town as my girlfriend, I'm the one who has to stick around and field the questions about what happened after you're gone."

"Fine, then don't," I said, harshly enough to make Violet look up at me in surprise. "We'll just keep hiding out here at the cabin so I can slink back to Boston without your family ever knowing we were together."

"That's not what I want," she said with a frustrated sigh.

"If you want to take me to the wedding as your friend, I'll go," I told her. "Because I *am* your friend, or at least I hope I am. I hope I'm more than that too."

"You're both," she said quietly. "Let's just play it by ear, okay?"

"Fine," I agreed, but our words buzzed like gnats in the air between us. I wanted more. I suspected she did too, but she was afraid to say so. Could we have more? Or was she smart to keep our relationship under wraps to protect herself after I'd left town?

Beside us, Violet slept on the blanket next to Cherry, who had flopped on her side and passed out in a milk coma, little paws twitching with puppy dreams. I envied the simplicity of her life, despite her dramatic start. Yesterday, she'd gone for a checkup, and the vet was cautiously optimistic that her liver troubles were behind her.

Every morning, Taylor picked up Minnie and went to work at the shelter before bringing Minnie back to her sister's house so she could come home to me in the evenings, and it was all amazingly good, despite the undercurrent of awkwardness over our future.

"Want to watch a movie tonight?" I hadn't found much time to sit around and watch movies when I was in Boston. There were a lot of things I hadn't made time for, like cuddling puppies or singing in a bar or helping a small-town bakery owner figure out where she could cut corners to improve her profit margins and hire the part-time help she desperately needed.

I was calmer and happier now than I'd been in...maybe ever. And Taylor was a big part of my newfound happiness. So was Violet. The puppies weren't exactly calming, but they did make me smile a lot. And for now, I was doing my best to enjoy every moment and trust that this was all going to work out the way it was meant to.

On Saturday, I put on a knee-length green dress that I'd brought with me to Vermont and that Taylor assured me was fancy enough for Steven's wedding. I put my hair up in a twist with a few loose curls to frame my face and did my makeup for maybe the fifth time since I'd been here. I'd gotten used to a more casual lifestyle, and I was discovering that I liked it.

Taylor had spent the morning at her apartment, catching up with Minnie, and had gotten ready there. She'd pick me up in about fifteen minutes, and Holly was coming over to stay with the puppies so they didn't get into trouble while I was out. Unofficially, she was also picking out which one she wanted to adopt.

I spritzed a little bit of perfume on my wrists and fastened my favorite necklace around my neck. It went perfectly with the low-cut neckline of this dress. Then I slipped into a pair of strappy flats since the ceremony took place in a park and I'd never mastered the art of walking in the grass while wearing heels.

"All right, you guys," I said as I scooped puppies out of the playpen into the laundry basket that had become their method of transport. A few days ago, Taylor had brought over a larger playpen that we'd set up in the backyard so that they could run around in an enclosed area. Otherwise, they darted off in every direction, and it was impossible to keep my eyes on all of them at once.

I put Sunny, Blaze, and Elizabeth in the basket and brought them out the back door with Violet at my heels. I didn't need a leash with her while the puppies were outside, because she never strayed far. She'd sit beside the playpen like a watchful mama. Cherry wasn't allowed to roughhouse with her siblings yet, but her staples came out in a few days, and she'd be allowed to rejoin the fun then.

In the playpen, Elizabeth toppled Blaze while Sunny squatted to pee. They really were growing up fast, just as Taylor had warned. While they frolicked in the grass, I went back in for Cherry. I scooped her out of her box and carried her outside. Mindful of her incision, I'd started carrying her belly up like a human baby, and she seemed to have taken to it.

She lay in the crook of my arm wearing a pink shirt, all four paws sticking skyward, eyes bright and watchful, her body loose and relaxed as if she didn't have a care in the world.

"Oh, just look at her!"

I turned to find Holly standing there, one hand pressed against her chest, and I had a feeling which puppy she was going to choose. Actually, I hoped she did adopt Cherry, because I'd grown fond of both Holly and Cherry over the past month, and I'd love to see them wind up together. I set Cherry in the warm grass at my feet, and she bounced toward Holly. "She's a handful today, I've got to warn you," I told her.

As if to prove my point, Cherry pounced on...well, I wasn't sure what she was aiming for, but she face planted in the grass with her butt sticking up in the air. She had a thicker coat than her mom. They all did. Taylor had told me that while it was impossible to say what breed their dad was without a DNA test, it was starting to look like they might be part Lab.

"I can handle her," Holly said with a smile as she knelt in the grass beside Cherry. The puppy licked her leg, tiny tail wagging.

"Want me to help you bring them back inside before I leave?" I asked.

"Nah," Holly said. "I'm happy to stay outside with them for a bit."

"Okay. I'll just bring Violet in and feed her."

As if she knew what I'd said, the dog turned and followed me into the house, those brown eyes tracking my every move as I mixed her usual bowl of wet and dry puppy chow and set it on the floor.

"You're in for an unhappy surprise pretty soon," I told her as she began to scarf down her food. "Once the puppies are weaned, you'll have to start eating regular portions again."

I washed my hands so I didn't go to the wedding smelling like dog food. I'd just dried them when I saw Taylor coming up the front steps. She had on burgundy slacks and a white button-down top, and my heart gave a little kick in my chest at the sight.

"Hi," I said as she came in through the front door. "You look really nice." Her hair was more polished than usual, and she'd accented her eyes with mascara and a coppery eyeshadow that complimented her complexion.

"So do you." She pulled me in for a quick kiss, tugging at the hem of my dress. "Ready for this?"

"Totally ready. I love your family." I still wasn't sure whether I was attending as Taylor's date or her friend, but either way, I was looking forward to the chance to see her family. I hoped I was her date, though, because I was tired of hiding. I wanted to shout our relationship from the rooftops. I wanted *everyone* to know.

We went out back to say goodbye to Holly, who was sitting in the grass playing with the puppies. Then we were on our way to Taylor's SUV. She'd been quiet since she got here, and I hoped she didn't regret inviting me.

"I'm looking forward to this," I told her. "I've never been to a wedding this small and informal before. It seems really personal and meaningful."

"Really?" She glanced at me as she drove. "Because I would picture you having a big expensive wedding in the city."

"That's certainly what my parents would want," I agreed.

"What kind of wedding would *you* want?"

I shrugged, staring out the window as we passed the farm at the end of the road. Cows roamed the green grass, tails flicking from side to side. "I don't know," I told her. "I guess I'm not one of those girls who has her dream wedding all planned out."

"Prefer to keep things casual?" she asked, and I was starting to dislike the direction this conversation had taken. It almost felt like she was trying to pick a fight with me, like she wanted me to say I hated everything about marriage, proclaim my love for the city, and leave her. But I wasn't going to give her a fight, at least not today.

"I'm capable of love and marriage," I told her. "What about you?"

"Ready and waiting," she said.

"And what kind of wedding would you want?"

"Something small and casual like Steven and Jill's."

"It would suit you," I told her. "And I definitely see you

having dogs involved somehow. Like, I've seen pictures where the couple had their dog as the ring bearer. You should do that."

She darted a glance in my direction, her expression softer than it had been a few minutes before. "Yeah. I mean, I can't help envisioning all the possibilities for disaster when you add dogs to a wedding ceremony, but it does sound like me."

"Probably no worse than having kids in your ceremony, right?" I said.

"Right," she agreed. "And dogs are cuter."

We managed to keep the conversation light the rest of the way to the park where the wedding would be held. I saw about two dozen people already gathered on the grass, women in casual dresses like mine and men in polo shirts and khaki pants. I hadn't been lying when I told Taylor I had no idea what my wedding would look like, but I liked this. A city wedding sounded nice too, but I might like something small, maybe set against the waterfront.

And when I pictured it, my bride looked an awful lot like Taylor...

She parked the SUV, and we stepped out. I'd hoped she might take my hand or even wrap an arm around me as we walked toward the other guests, but she kept her hands to herself as we crossed the lawn. Obviously, we needed to have a chat about the future, and soon.

"Taylor," someone called, and we turned toward a couple I recognized as her parents. Aside from a few extra wrinkles, they looked more or less the same as I remembered, and I found myself smiling as we approached. I'd spent a lot of happy afternoons at their house when I was growing up.

"Mom, Dad, you remember Phoebe," Taylor said, still not touching me.

"Phoebe!" Taylor's mom exclaimed, throwing her arms out to hug me. "Well, if you aren't a sight for sore eyes. Look at you!" She wrapped me in a tight embrace.

"It's good to see you too, Mrs. Donovan," I told her.

"Oh, please call me Debbie. We're all adults now," she said with a laugh, reminding me why I'd always liked her. "I'd heard you were back in town. It's so good to see you again."

"You too," I told her. "I'm so glad to be back."

"Such a shame about your grandma," Debbie said, giving her head a shake. "We were all just devastated when she passed away."

"Thank you," I said.

"Taylor says she's got you fostering a litter of puppies?" her mom asked.

"She does, and they're quite a handful," I told her with a laugh.

"Which is why I've been spending plenty of time helping you with them," Taylor said, speaking for the first time since she'd introduced me to her parents.

"Well, it's great to see you, Phoebe. I'm so glad you came with Taylor tonight." Debbie glanced between us, and if I wasn't mistaken, she seemed to put two and two together, perhaps alerted by the awkward way Taylor was acting. The two of them had always been close, or at least they had when Taylor was younger, and I assumed they still were.

"It's great to see you too," I told her.

We chatted for a few more minutes, and then everyone began making their way over to the rows of white chairs that faced the gazebo in front of the lake. It was a beautiful backdrop. Steven wore a gray suit with a red rose pinned over the breast pocket, looking appropriately misty-eyed as the big moment approached.

Taylor and I sat with her family, having been joined by her sister Kelly, her brother Luke, and their spouses. They all greeted me warmly, which was great, but the longer I sat here, the more this started to feel like high school, when Taylor and I had hidden our relationship behind the mask of our friendship. It had been necessary then, since I was still in the closet, but now it just felt awkward. I wanted to hold her hand, and I wanted to dance with her after the ceremony.

Kelly asked me questions about Boston while we waited for the ceremony to start. She and her husband were visiting the city for a mini-vacation next month and wanted all my suggestions for what to see and do while they were in town. I had plenty of them, sharing recommendations until music began to play behind us, alerting us to the start of the ceremony.

I turned in my seat to see the bride in a simple white dress, carrying a bouquet of brightly colored flowers. A ripple of excitement passed through the crowd, murmurs and whispers about how beautiful she looked. But when I looked at Taylor, I was surprised to find her watching me instead of the bride.

28

TAYLOR

Phoebe was so beautiful tonight, I couldn't take my eyes off her. As we made our way to the bar after the ceremony, I found myself watching the way the afternoon sun glinted in her hair and how perfectly the green of her dress complemented her complexion. That dress…

It fell to her knees, hugging her figure just enough to make my throat dry without being overtly sexy. The neckline plunged in the front, causing me to fantasize about what kind of bra—if any—she might be wearing underneath. I was definitely going to find out when we got home, which would hopefully be soon.

I didn't plan to stay at the reception very long. It was torture having her here without telling everyone I knew that this was the woman I loved, the only woman I'd *ever* loved. And what was the point, when she was about to leave town?

"What do you want to drink?" I asked her as we reached the front of the line. I saw a big bowl of some kind of punch, along with a selection of wine and beer.

"Champagne punch?" the bartender asked.

"Yes, please," Phoebe said, extending a hand.

He handed her a glass of pink punch before turning to me.

"The same," I told him. I rarely drank wine, and champagne even less often, but it felt appropriate at a wedding.

We took our glasses and made our way across the grass toward my family, who had gathered at a table under the picnic shelter. Phoebe seemed at ease with them. Her smile looked genuine, and her shoulders were relaxed. I'd made things between us awkward earlier, but I didn't know how else to act. I didn't know how to protect my heart against her imminent departure, not when she looked at me like I was the only woman in the world and talked about simple weddings here in Vermont.

What was I supposed to think? And how was I supposed to let her go?

I didn't know the answer to either question. Instead, we sat and ate with my family. By the time the cake was cut, strands of lights overhead had been lit against the growing dusk and music began to play through the park, inviting us to dance. It was probably time for Phoebe and me to leave before the evening got any more complicated.

"I'll be right back," Phoebe said, brushing a hand against my waist before she headed in the direction of the bathrooms.

I made my way toward the bar to get some water, bumping into my mom on the way.

"Is it my imagination, or are you and Phoebe more than friends?" she asked as she fell into step beside me.

"Um." I gave her a look, partly annoyed that she'd noticed what I'd been too afraid to tell her, but mostly relieved that she'd called me on it. "Yeah, we are."

Mom beamed at me. "I thought I saw something between you tonight, and then I got to thinking about how close you were the summer after you came out. It didn't click for me then, but looking back…am I wrong?"

"You're not wrong," I told her.

She looked thoughtful for a moment. "Now I can't believe I missed it. You two were high school sweethearts? Why didn't you ever tell me?"

"Phoebe wasn't out then," I told her. "It wasn't my story to tell. We broke up at the end of the summer, and that was the end of it until she came back last month."

Mom tapped a finger against her lips. "So that's why you two quit speaking. I always wondered."

"That's why."

"And now you're back together," she said. "Is it serious?"

"I don't know." And that was basically the whole problem. "I think it could be…but she's headed back to Boston soon, so I just don't see a future for us."

"There's no possibility of her staying?"

"I don't think so."

"Sounds like you two need to have a talk about it." Mom shifted her gaze to look over my shoulder, letting me know that Phoebe was on her way back. Sure enough, she slid in beside me a few moments later, and this time, I took her hand. It seemed pointless to deny what my mom—and who knew who else—had already figured out.

"Want to dance?" I asked her.

Her whole expression brightened. "I'd love to."

We excused ourselves from my mom and walked to the part of the lawn where other couples were dancing. There wasn't a dance floor, so we were limited by our ability to dance on grass, but Phoebe and I were up for the challenge. After a few minutes, a ballad began to play, and we moved closer to each other.

"I'm sorry I was trying to hold you at arm's length tonight," I said as I took her hands in mine, tugging her in for a kiss as we began to sway to the music.

Her eyes widened, reflecting the bulbs overhead like stars in the night sky. "Well, I'm glad you changed your mind."

"Me too." I slid an arm around her waist, and she settled against me, her cheek resting against mine, or more like against the side of my chin. Our height difference was more pronounced when she wore flats.

"What changed your mind?" she asked, looking up at me.

"I hated not touching you, for one thing," I told her. "But also, my mom figured it out anyway."

Phoebe's lips curved in a smile before she ducked her head, resting it in the crook of my neck. "Why does that not surprise me?"

"She's pretty observant," I agreed.

"And you're okay with it?"

"Sure. It's not like I didn't want people to know we're together. I just...I'm scared of you leaving."

"Well, I'm not leaving tonight," she said quietly. "I might not leave at all if you'd quit pushing me away."

"What?" I drew back to look at her.

She met my gaze head-on. "Things will have to change, it's true. I don't own the cabin, and my dad's getting antsy for me to finish up so he can rent it out. Not to mention, I'm paying for a condo in Boston that's sitting empty. But change doesn't have to be a bad thing, and it certainly doesn't mean we have to break up."

"I want to believe that." With my hands resting on her waist, the warmth of her body beneath my fingers, and the full force of those chocolate eyes on mine, I wanted forever with this woman.

"Then let's just go with the flow and see what happens," she said.

"I don't know if that's enough for me, but I'm trying."

"What part of it isn't enough?" she asked.

"The part where you go back to Boston, whenever and however it happens."

"I'm trying to tell you that maybe I won't go," she whispered, pressing a kiss against my neck. "I'd have to find a job here...and a home, and those are big things to think about when you and I have only been together a few weeks. I won't make promises I can't keep, but I want to make this work, Taylor."

I pulled her closer. "I'm sorry for pushing you away earlier."

"I know you're afraid of getting hurt," she said. "But don't you see that I'm afraid of the same thing? This is scary for me too.

Boston is my home. I don't know if I can build a life for myself here in Vermont, but I'm trying."

"And I really appreciate that," I said. "Because I know I could never live in Boston."

"Not even for me?" She rested her head on my shoulder, peering up at me.

"I could say yes," I told her, deciding to be as honest with her as she'd just been with me. "I could move to Boston, but I'd never truly be happy there, and sooner or later, it would poison our relationship."

"Fair enough," she said. "Well, I love Boston, and my friends and family are there, but I like it here too. I can't get the same kind of job here that I had there, but I could expand my job search to the Burlington area and see if there's anything here that could work."

"Really? You'd do that for me?"

She smiled, wrapping her arms around me as we swayed to the music. "Yeah, I would."

My throat tightened, and tears glazed my vision. "That's a pretty big deal, Phoebe Shaw."

"I know, and like I said, I'm not making any promises. I'm just keeping all my options open right now, okay?"

I nodded, feeling hopeful for the first time since she'd come back into my life. "Okay."

I woke in Phoebe's bed the next morning, wrapped in the welcome warmth of her body. Except...Phoebe wasn't usually a snuggler. Since I'd started sleeping here after Cherry's surgery, I'd generally woken on one side of the bed, while she was curled on the other. I opened my eyes to discover Violet pressed against me, fast asleep with her head on the pillow. "Oh boy," I whispered.

"What?" Phoebe mumbled from the far side of the bed.

"I think someone's ready to join the adults." I reached out to rub Violet. Her eyes popped open, and her tail started wagging.

Phoebe's arm slid around my waist as she rolled to face me. "Oh my God. What is she doing in the bed?"

"Her bed is full of small nursing creatures who've got their baby teeth in now?" I suggested, giving Violet another rub.

"Yikes," Phoebe murmured. "Do they bite her when they nurse?"

"I don't know, but they're old enough that it's fine for her to want some time away from them."

The puppies were cute, but they were kind of a mood killer, because instead of fooling around in bed with Phoebe like I wanted to, we had to get up and take them outside. Even so, the pads in the whelping pen were a mess and had to be swapped out. Four weeks old was a challenging age. They were old enough to play, almost ready to start eating solid food, and they could go to the bathroom on their own now but weren't old enough to have any real bladder control.

"Yuck," Phoebe said, echoing my thoughts as we cleaned out the pen together. "No wonder Violet got in bed with us. I wouldn't want to sleep in here either."

The situation was made more complicated by Cherry, who still had to be separated from the rest of her siblings unless one of us could supervise. The good news was that she'd get her staples out in two days. The bad news was that her current T-shirt was soaked in pee. I removed it and carried her outside to see if she'd pee again on her own before I cleaned her up.

Then I bottle fed her while Phoebe took the other puppies outside. By the time I'd finished, Phoebe had started a pot of coffee and gated the puppies in the kitchen with her, where they were currently rolling each other across the floor, yipping and playing. Violet was on the other side of the room, eating her breakfast.

"I liked them better when they stayed in one place," Phoebe

said, brushing a curl out of her face with the back of her hand. "This is insanity."

"It is," I agreed. "But it only lasts a few weeks."

"I don't know why anyone would voluntarily sign up for this." She narrowed her eyes at the puppies.

"Because they're cute?" I scooped Blaze off the floor and held him out to her. He wriggled in my hands, leaning forward to lick her face.

She smiled, shaking her head. "They're cute, but oh my God, please grow up already so we can send them to their new homes."

"Soon." I was already fielding adoption applications for them and hoped to finalize their forever homes in the next week or so. I'd been dragging my feet a bit, waiting for Holly to make her pick, knowing I wouldn't have trouble placing the other three. Puppies were easy that way. Violet would be harder to place, but if she and Minnie got along, I could take her in as my new foster after the puppies were weaned, unless Phoebe was still here.

If Phoebe was still here. If Phoebe wanted to keep fostering her.

If…

Last night, she'd sounded like she wanted to stay. This morning, she was side-eyeing the puppies in her kitchen like she couldn't get out of here fast enough. I'd basically moved in with her after Cherry's surgery, and now I was hesitant to leave, since I'd brought this puppy chaos into her life. Maybe Kelly could keep Minnie until these guys were fully weaned.

But what would happen after the puppies were adopted?

29

PHOEBE

The next three weeks passed in a blur of puppy-related chaos. There were holes chewed in blankets, pee-soaked floors, and a plenty of super-cute antics that at least partly made up for the mess and destruction. Cherry got her staples out and rejoined her siblings with a clean bill of health, and Holly made her adoption official. She'd be going home on Friday. They all would. Taylor had worked hard to find amazing homes for them.

In the meantime, I'd gone on several job interviews—two in-person here in the Burlington area and three Skype interviews for positions in Boston. One of those virtual interviews had landed me a follow-up in Boston next Wednesday that I'd have to drive down for. The position was exactly what I was looking for, except that it would take me away from Vermont.

Between singing at V and V, doing consulting work for local business owners, and fostering for Taylor, I'd become a much bigger part of the community here than I'd expected to. None of it was what I'd thought I wanted, but I was happy. I'd be relaxed too if I didn't currently have a puppy chewing on the cuff of my pants.

"Knock it off, Elizabeth," I said as I removed her little teeth from my jeans, zigzagging my way across the kitchen to avoid puppy paws. The cabin was ready for rental now. I'd finished decorating it this week, and since I kept the puppies gated in the kitchen most of the time, nothing had gotten ruined...at least, not yet.

Once they left, it would be time for me to move out too. My dad was anxious to start renting the place. He was tired of paying utilities and upkeep here without earning anything back, and I could hardly blame him.

Taylor was on her way over, and I was trying to get a casserole in the oven for us, but my furry cohorts were getting in the way. Violet lay on her dog bed in the living room, fast asleep. Now that they were weaned, she was spending more and more time away from them. She'd become a regular presence in my bed at night. Taylor had also become a regular presence in my bed, and I hoped that might continue, even if we weren't sleeping in this house.

I covered the casserole pan with aluminum foil and bent to slide it into the oven. Blaze lunged at my hair, and I winced at the sharp tug of his teeth.

"You guys are little hooligans," I muttered as I disentangled him from my hair and stood. "Really cute hooligans, but hooligans nonetheless." My phone rang, and I turned to grab it from the table. "Hi, Dad."

"Hi, honey. How are you?" he asked, and I could hear the sound of Boston traffic over the line, along with an echo that let me know I was on speaker in his car.

"I'm ready for these puppies to go to their forever homes, but other than that, I'm great. And the cabin's ready to rent, if that's why you're calling. I'll have it fully staged and puppy-free for the photographer you hired next week."

"About that," he said, and there was something apologetic in his tone that made me stand up a little straighter. "Is Taylor still interested in buying?"

I let myself out of the kitchen through the baby gate and dropped onto the couch across from Violet. "Um, I think she would be. Why?"

"I mentioned her offer offhand to Vivian, and she thinks I should sell." He sighed, and I fought the urge to roll my eyes. He really was whipped where his new wife was concerned. "Apparently, she's always wanted a condo in the Bahamas, and we could afford it if I sold the cabin."

"So now you want to sell?" I rubbed a hand over my brow. This didn't make sense. My dad loved this house, which was why he'd been so determined to hold on to it. And while I wanted Taylor to have the chance to buy it, I also didn't want my dad to do anything he'd regret.

"I've given it some thought, and I'm not getting any younger, you know? I don't get up to Vermont as often as I'd like, and dealing with renters might be more of a hassle than it's worth. Selling to Taylor would be easy and quick, and I know the cabin would be going to someone who will love and care for it the way your grandma would have wanted."

"Wow, Dad. I don't know what to say." I leaned forward, resting my elbows on my knees. This was what Taylor had wanted, and the thought of being able to give it to her filled me with a mixture of happiness and something else...something vaguely sad. As I looked around the living room, I realized this place had started to feel like home over the last two months, and I was unexpectedly nostalgic at the thought of giving it up.

Of course, I'd always been leaving, but as long as the property stayed in the family, at least there would have been the possibility of visiting. Well, if Taylor and I stayed together, that possibility remained. But right now, everything felt upside down and confusing.

"Talk to her, will you?" my dad asked. "And if she's interested, give her my number. If she's willing to pay a fair market price, we should be able to negotiate the sale without having to get Realtors involved."

"Okay," I said. "You're sure this isn't a midlife crisis?"

He chuckled, and I heard the sound of the blinker as he signaled a turn. "It's possible, sweetie, but I'm sure nonetheless.

I've got so many air miles saved up, I don't know what to do with them. A little sun and sand will be good for me, don't you think?"

"Yeah," I said, smiling at the mental image. My dad did need to slow down. He needed a vacation. Maybe a condo in the Bahamas would be good for him. "I'll talk to Taylor."

"Let me know what she decides," he said.

"Will do."

We wrapped up the call, and I sat there for a few minutes afterward, just staring at the phone in my hands. Taylor would get to buy this place after all. Would I stay? Would I go? This wasn't my house. It had never been, even if it had started to feel like it. And now I'd spent two months fixing it up and dressing it for renters that would never come.

I'd left Boston desperate for a place to hide, a distraction from the stupid meme that had derailed my life, and I'd found it here in this cabin. I hadn't expected Violet or her puppies, and I certainly hadn't expected Taylor to come back into my life.

Now, it was time to move on and figure out what came next. The puppies would go to their new homes, and Taylor would move in here permanently. "You and I need new homes, Violet," I said to the dog.

She looked up at me, tail wagging lazily against her dog bed.

On cue, I heard Taylor coming in through the front door. She dropped her purse on the counter and bypassed the kitchen to greet me with a kiss. "Hey."

"Hi." I stood, wrapping my arms around her. "Want to help me take them out back?"

"Sure." She crossed the room and opened the baby gate, and I helped shepherd the four furry tornadoes out the back door. We herded them into their outdoor playpen, where they took turns peeing and wrestling. Little heathens.

I smiled as I watched them. "I have some interesting news for you."

"Yeah?" The look she gave me was sharper than I'd expected. "You got a job?"

I shook my head. "My news is for *you*, actually."

A wrinkle appeared between her brows as she waited for me to explain.

"My dad had a change of heart. He wants to sell this place to you and buy a condo in the Bahamas for himself and Vivian instead."

"What?" Taylor pressed a hand over her mouth. "No way. Really?"

"Really. You still want to buy it, right?"

"I do," she said, eyes widening. "I really do."

"Then it's yours," I told her.

"What happened to change his mind?" she asked, glancing around the yard like she was already envisioning herself living here. "And why a condo in the Bahamas?"

I repeated my dad's story, and Taylor's smile grew while she listened.

"Wow. That's crazy," she said. "And amazing."

Before I knew it, she'd pulled me into her arms. With a laugh, she spun me while I clung to her with a surprised giggle. She looked ecstatic, like I'd just given her everything she'd ever wanted. And while I was a little unsure where I fit into this new scenario, I was happy for her, *really* happy for her.

"My grandma would be so happy about this," I told her. "I really think she would be thrilled to have you and your dogs living here."

"I hope so," Taylor said, her eyes suspiciously glossy. "I mean, I think so too, but it means more coming from you, as her grand-daughter."

"I think you can trust your own judgment where she's concerned."

Taylor reached out to tuck a lock of my hair behind my ear, her fingers lingering against my neck. "And you?"

"I'm happy you'll be living here too," I told her.

"No, I mean, what does this mean for you?" She threaded her fingers with mine.

"I don't know," I said. "That's up to you, I guess. Why don't you give my dad a call and work out the details, and then you and I can take it from there?"

"I'd like you to stay," she said, her expression gone serious.

"We'll see, okay? I've freeloaded in this house long enough. It's time for me to find my own place, depending on what job I get and where." I wanted to stay. I wanted it more than anything, but I couldn't let her buy this house with her hard-earned money and then live here like a guest. This was a scenario I hadn't planned for, and I wasn't sure how to handle it.

Taylor turned away like I'd hurt her feelings. "You're probably right."

Whatever happened, I had to decide soon, because I needed to sell my condo in Boston if I wasn't going to live there. But first, I needed a job. "Dinner's almost ready," I told her. "And afterward, you can give my dad a call and make things official."

30
TAYLOR

It was an awkward dinner. On the one hand, I couldn't stop smiling. This cabin was my dream home. I'd live within walking distance of my parents' house. I could foster as many dogs as I wanted—within reason, of course. And I'd get to make my home in a place where I already had so many happy memories.

Phoebe had been quiet since she told me the news, her expression hesitant, as if she wasn't sure where she belonged anymore. A part of me felt like I was kicking her out of her house, even though she'd never planned to live here.

Once I bought it, she'd be a guest in her grandmother's cabin, but what was the alternative? I couldn't ask her to sell her condo in Boston and buy a house with me two months after coming back into her life. That would be premature and presumptuous, and she didn't even have a job yet. So we shared stilted dinner conversation while we ate chicken cordon bleu casserole, and I hoped the answer would present itself to me before it was too late.

In the kitchen, one of the puppies let out a loud yip, and Phoebe rolled her eyes, displaying the playful annoyance that was her usual reaction to them. She loved them, but she was ready for them to go to their forever homes, and I couldn't blame her. They were a lot to handle.

"I think we could try introducing Minnie and Violet soon," I told her.

"Oh yeah?" She glanced across the table at me. "That would simplify things, wouldn't it?"

I nodded. "What if I bring Minnie over for a hike tomorrow, and you join us with Violet? I know she's not in shape to go far, but meeting outside on neutral ground, away from the puppies, should be a good way to make an introduction between them."

Phoebe nodded. "Let's do it."

The next day, I drove straight to Phoebe's house—soon to be my house—after work with Minnie in tow. I texted Phoebe when I arrived and then brought Minnie around back. We crossed the stream and headed onto the path so that she wouldn't be meeting Violet on her own territory. I kept her on leash today so Violet wouldn't feel ambushed.

A few minutes later, Phoebe appeared on the trail with Violet at her side. The dog stiffened when she caught sight of Minnie, and the hair along her spine raised in alarm.

"It's okay," Phoebe soothed, keeping a tight grip on the leash. "This is Taylor's dog. We're hoping you two might be friends."

Minnie tugged at her leash, tail wagging enthusiastically. She'd never met a dog she didn't want to be best friends with, so today's success or failure would be up to Violet.

"Let's start walking," I suggested.

Phoebe fell into step beside me with Violet on her other side, and we walked for a few minutes, talking casually while the dogs stole glances at each other around our legs. By the time we'd reached the top of the hill, Violet was relaxed, tail up and tongue out.

"I think you can let them greet now," I told Phoebe. "Don't tense up. Just follow her lead. If anything starts to look bad, I'll move Minnie out of reach."

"Got it," she said, looking nervous. Her nerves weren't helping, but it wasn't like I could just tell her not to worry. Luckily, Violet didn't seem ruffled. She leaned forward and sniffed Minnie, who immediately took the opportunity to come around and sniff Violet's butt. They sniffed and circled each other for a minute, and then I gestured to Phoebe that we should keep walking.

"We'll turn around in a minute," I told Phoebe. "I don't want Violet to overdo it when she's not used to hiking and still carrying some baby weight."

"This is going really well," Phoebe said as we reversed direction on the trail.

"It is," I agreed. "We'll do it again, and after the puppies are adopted, we can see how Violet feels about having Minnie in the house."

"Who will take her after I move out?" Phoebe asked, looking at Violet, and the sadness in her eyes was unmistakable.

"Hopefully, I will," I told her. "If they get along, I'll foster her until she's been spayed and adopted."

"Good," Phoebe said, nodding her approval. "I love that idea."

"Will you stay too?" I asked. "Until you find a job and decide what you're doing long-term?"

"For now," she said. "But I have to pay rent or something. I can't just crash in your house indefinitely."

"Well, I want you to crash here until you find a job. We'll figure out the rest afterward."

"Okay," she agreed, still looking hesitant. "Thank you."

We approached the back of the house, and I stopped Minnie at the creek. "Mind if I go home with her tonight? It's been a while."

"Oh, yeah, sure," Phoebe said, fingers curling around Violet's leash. "I can manage the puppies for a night."

"Thanks. I haven't spent a night at my place in a few weeks, and Kelly's ready for a break from watching Minnie. Not to mention, I need to start going through all my stuff and packing." This morning, I'd talked to Mr. Shaw, and we'd agreed on a price and sales terms. We hoped to have all the paperwork taken care of within the next week or so. Luckily, I had a lawyer friend who was going to look over the contract for me, since we weren't involving Realtors. I wasn't expecting any trouble, though. Phoebe's dad was an honest and fair man, as far as I knew.

She leaned in to give me a kiss. "I'll see you tomorrow, then?"

"You sure will. It's puppy adoption day." We grinned at each other.

"Thank *God*," she said dramatically.

"Oh, come on. You're going to miss them," I teased.

"Not even a little bit. After this experience, I can safely say I'm never getting a puppy."

"Well, you've done a great job with them," I told her. "And what about Violet? You two seem pretty fond of each other."

Phoebe looked down at the pit bull. "I like this girl a lot. I hope she and Minnie get along well enough for us all to live together until she's adopted and I find a job."

I wanted to suggest that *she* adopt Violet, but that seemed pushy, when she hadn't even decided to stay in Vermont yet. Pets weren't allowed in her condo in Boston. She'd been clear about that, and a condo was no place for a dog Violet's size anyway.

I took Minnie home, and we shared a quiet evening together, one of the last nights we'd ever share in this apartment. Minnie was overjoyed to be back at home with me. We had dinner together and played with her tug toy for a while, and that night, she curled up in bed beside me, the way she'd always done.

The next morning, we got ready together and headed to the shelter. I was only working in the office until noon today because the afternoon would be spent on puppy adoptions, which I would be completing at the cabin. I hadn't seen a reason to bring them into the shelter when I could bring the paperwork with me to Phoebe's house.

My house.

I still couldn't quite believe it was going to be my house. I spent a quiet morning at my desk, updating the online profiles for our available pets. Violet's puppies were currently listed as "adoption pending," and if all went as planned, I could change that to "adopted" in about an hour. I gathered the adoption paperwork and set out for the cabin, leaving Minnie with Alleya for the afternoon.

"Hey," Phoebe said as she greeted me at the door. Her hair was up, and her cheeks were flushed, likely from puppy wrangling.

"Ready to send these guys home?" I asked as I gave her a quick kiss.

"You know, I think I might miss them a *tiny* bit once they're gone," she said, giving the puppies an affectionate look.

I followed her gaze, noticing that she'd tied little bows around their necks, and my heart melted into a hopeless puddle right then and there. Elizabeth's bow was pink, while Cherry wore a cherry-red one. Sunny's was a sunny yellow, and Blaze's was bright blue. As they romped around the kitchen, wrestling with each other, the overall effect was too adorable for words. "That is one of the cutest things I've ever seen."

Phoebe beamed at me. "Thanks. I thought they should look good for their new families. I bathed them and everything. I also think we should take them to the pen in back before their families get here so their first impression isn't of their new puppy having an accident on the floor."

"Great idea." I bent to scoop up Sunny and Elizabeth while she lifted the other two, and we headed out the back door with them. Violet followed us. She watched as we put the puppies into their pen before settling contentedly in the grass nearby. "You've been such a good mama, Violet. I bet you're going to be lonely tonight without them around."

"I bet she'll be relieved too," Phoebe said with a laugh. "She's definitely been enjoying more time away from them lately."

"I would too if I had four babies trying to nurse on me all the time." I walked to the table on the patio and pulled out the four folders I'd brought home with me, one for each puppy. I got everything ready for the adopters while Phoebe went inside to clean up in case anyone needed to go in the house.

"That was the last time I have to clean up puppy pee," she announced as she came back out a few minutes later. "And if I start to feel sad about saying goodbye to them, just remind me of that fact, because I am *so* over the pee."

"And the poop," I agreed. The sound of tires crunching over gravel in the driveway reached us at the same time, and Phoebe gave me a nervous smile. "I'll go greet them," I told her. "You stay with the puppies so no one gets tangled in their bow."

I walked around to the front of the house, where a tall man was getting out of his car. This was Brody Reynolds, one of the vet techs who'd seen the puppies for their checkups. He had the first appointment of the afternoon, and coincidentally, he was here to adopt our firstborn puppy, Elizabeth. "Hi, Brody," I said.

"Hey, Taylor."

I led him around the side of the house. "I'm sure you recognize her, but she's in the pink bow."

"She's hard to miss," he said, smiling broadly as Elizabeth bounded across the playpen to topple Blaze. He walked over to greet her, rubbing her head while she attempted to chew on his fingers, and then we sat at the table to fill out the adoption paperwork.

A few minutes later, he was on his way back to his car with Elizabeth tucked under his arm. Phoebe watched with a somewhat wistful expression, but whatever she was feeling was tempered by the arrival of the next family—sisters from the local university who were here to adopt Sunny. They cooed over him as they signed the paperwork, arguing good naturedly over who would drive home and who got to hold the puppy.

Next up was the young couple who was adopting Blaze. They'd bought him a fancy matching collar and leash to wear home and were already snapping happy selfies with him before they made it to the car. Last but certainly not least, Holly arrived to pick up Cherry. Her senior dog had passed away two weeks ago, and she'd been doting on Cherry extra hard in the weeks since.

"I'll miss you, little one," Phoebe said, lifting the puppy to give her a squeeze. Cherry kissed her face enthusiastically. We'd spent so much extra time with Cherry, nursing her back to health after her surgery. I'd still get to see her since Holly volunteered at the shelter, but Phoebe...well, it depended on whether she stayed.

We sent Holly and Cherry on their way, and then it was just me, Phoebe, and Violet left in the backyard. Violet stood beside the empty playpen, whining softly.

"Aw, she's sad," Phoebe said, pressing a hand over her heart.

"Let's take her for a walk," I suggested. "She'll be a little sad this evening, but she'll be just fine. In fact, her personality may start to really blossom now that she's on the receiving end of all the attention instead of having to share us with her puppies."

"I hope so." Phoebe ducked inside for Violet's leash, and we led her over the stream and onto the path. Violet sniffed as she walked, not looking particularly upset to be without her puppies. "When will we try to bring Minnie over?"

"Let's give Violet a day or two to adjust to life without her babies first."

"Sounds like a good idea." Phoebe looked at the dog and then at me. "And then, don't forget I have an interview in Boston on Wednesday."

"Right." I hadn't forgotten. On the contrary, I was terrified she'd drive to Boston and decide she didn't want to come back. And what if she got the job? Then she'd have to stay.

"Even if I get the job, it doesn't mean I'm leaving Vermont permanently," she said, obviously having read the direction my thoughts had taken.

"Doesn't it?" I countered. It was only a three-hour drive between here and Boston, but combined with our work schedules and my dogs, we'd be lucky to see each other every weekend. Probably, we'd only see each other a few times a month, and would that be enough?

"If things between us keep going the way they're going, I'll keep interviewing here in Burlington, even if I get the job in Boston, okay?" She took my hand, giving it a reassuring squeeze. "I just need to feel out my options."

"Right," I said, but I wasn't sure I believed it. Now that the puppies were gone and I'd bought the cabin, there was nothing keeping Phoebe in Vermont, and I was terrified that she'd realize it. "Well, I'll try to get Minnie and Violet acclimated to each other before you leave, and then I'll stay here with them while you're gone."

She nodded. "It's only for one night, Taylor. I'm coming back."

31

PHOEBE

I strode down Boylston Street on Wednesday afternoon, cell phone in hand, as the wind tossed my hair in my face and my heels thumped against the concrete. I'd just come from my interview with Bellair Innovations, and I was cautiously optimistic that it had gone well, although it was hard to know for sure. After more than two months away from Boston and the corporate world, it all felt a bit like culture shock now.

Consequently, I felt vaguely out of sorts as I walked toward the nearest T station to catch the subway back to my condo. I missed Violet, who wasn't even my dog. I missed the cabin that wasn't my house. And I missed Taylor...who maybe could be mine, if I found a way to give up my life here and move to Vermont permanently.

The meme that had driven me out of the city felt like a distant memory now. I'd only been back for a few hours, but no one had given me a second glance, and when I'd dared to reinstall Twitter on my phone, my notifications had gone silent weeks ago. No one was talking about "girl against the patriarchy" anymore. If I wanted my old life back, it was mine for the taking, especially if I got this job. But *did* I want it back?

I boarded the subway and slumped into an available seat, closing my eyes as the train began to move. Wheels screeched against the rails, and the seat rattled beneath me, submersing me in the familiar sounds and sensations of Boston. I'd missed this. As much as I missed the things I'd left behind in Vermont, I loved it here. I loved the convenience of the subway and my favorite restaurants and going out with my friends whenever I wanted.

When I walked into my condo thirty minutes later, it felt an awful lot like coming home. How would I reconcile my life here with my life there? Could Vermont be enough for me? I went into my bedroom to ransack my closet for something fun to wear tonight. I was having drinks with my two best friends, Courtney and Emily, and I could hardly wait to see them.

After wearing the same suitcase worth of clothes for over two months in Vermont, the freedom to pick something different today was thrilling. I put on dressy jeans and a sleek red blouse that had always been one of my favorites. Then I touched up my makeup, going extra smokey on the eye shadow and heavy on the eyeliner. I was overdue for a night out with my friends, dammit.

Before I headed out, I took a selfie in front of the window in my living room with the Boston skyline visible behind me and texted it to Taylor with a bunch of x's and o's. I wished she could be here with me tonight. She said she hated the city, but I couldn't imagine anyone truly hating an occasional night here.

Fancy drinks, lots of laughter, and maybe a stroll through some of my favorite spots in the city before I headed back to my condo tonight? It felt pretty perfect to me. As I picked up my purse and headed for the door, Taylor replied with a selfie of herself sitting on the couch in my grandmother's cabin—Taylor's cabin now—with Minnie on one side of her and Violet on the other.

My heart ached at the sight. *Can't wait to see all 3 of you tomorrow,* I texted back.

Before I made it out the door, my phone started to ring with an unknown Boston number, and my pulse kicked into overdrive. It was probably too soon to hear back about the job, but... "Hello?"

"Is this Phoebe Shaw?" a woman's voice asked.

"Yes, it is." I pressed a hand against the kitchen counter, bracing myself.

"Hi, Phoebe, it's Allison Renwald from Bellair Innovations."

Butterflies flapped in my stomach. I'd just interviewed with Allison an hour ago, and she'd told me they were looking to move quickly on this position, but even so, I hadn't expected to hear *this* quickly, and now my knees were shaking. "Hi, Allison," I managed, sounding breathless.

"I have some good news for you," she told me. "We were very impressed with your prior experience in the financial sector, and everyone on the team enjoyed meeting with you today. I confess I rushed things through since I know you're headed to Vermont tomorrow, and I wanted to have you come back in before you leave to go over salary and details if you're interested, because you've got the job."

"Oh," I said, staring out my window at the Boston skyline, so different from the thick trees and rolling hills I'd gotten used to. "Wow, Allison. I don't know what to say. I'm floored. Thank you so much."

"I know you'll want to take some time to think it over," she said. "I'll email you with the full details of our offer, including the benefits package. And if you're ready to accept tomorrow morning, please come in before you drive back to Vermont. If not, we'll handle it later virtually."

"Okay, I'll look it over and get back to you before I leave tomorrow," I told her. When I hung up the phone a few minutes later, I stood in my kitchen for several long minutes, just staring out the window. I couldn't say no to an opportunity like this, but it didn't mean I was tied to Boston forever either. I could keep looking for a job in Burlington in the meantime, and I could drive up to see Taylor on the weekends. We could make it work.

Speaking of Taylor, I picked up my phone and dialed her.

"Missing me already?" she asked when she answered.

"Always, and I also have news."

"You got the job." She said it matter-of-factly, as if she'd known this was going to happen. Maybe she had, but I hadn't.

"I did."

"Congratulations," she said, but her voice was flat.

"Thank you." My stomach twisted uncomfortably. I was so excited about my new job. Truly, it was exactly what I wanted to be doing, the kind of job that would be so hard to find in Vermont, where there weren't many large financial firms.

"I guess that's that, then," she said.

"What's what?" I asked, rubbing a hand over my brow.

"You're back in Boston."

"For tonight," I told her.

"You're not taking the job, then?" Taylor asked.

"I am, but that doesn't mean we can't still see each other. I'll drive up on weekends, and I can keep feelers out for a job in Burlington. If things seem to be going in the right direction for us, then I can still move later on."

"I don't know if I can do long-distance," Taylor said, and I heard the anguish in her voice. It brought tears to my eyes. "I just…I feel like I'm losing you all over again."

"But you're not," I insisted. "I live here in Boston, Taylor. I've always lived here. I'm trying to find a way to bridge the gap, to stay with you, to transition my life to Vermont if the opportunity arises, but you just have to be patient with me while I figure it out."

"I know you are. I just don't know if it will be enough for me." Her voice cracked. "I'm a simple, small-town girl, Phoebe. All I want is you and this little cabin and a house full of dogs."

"You can have all of that." I blinked to clear my vision. "You already have it."

"I'm not so sure that I do."

"Jesus Christ." I started to pace then, treading a path around the living room. "I can't believe we're arguing about this, especially on the phone."

"You're right," Taylor said with a sigh. "We'll talk about it in person when you get back tomorrow, okay?"

"Fine." And because my feelings were hurt, I hung up the phone without saying goodbye.

———

"I'm so happy to see you, Phoebs," Courtney said as she sipped from her martini. "Between everything going on with the cabin and the puppies and your new relationship with Taylor, I wasn't sure you were coming back."

"I might not be," I admitted. "Everything's kind of up in the air right now."

"I want to be devastated about this, because I'll miss the hell out of you if you move, but I can't be sad about you being swept off your feet by a woman," Courtney said.

"Your high school sweetheart," Emily agreed. "It's so romantic."

"Your first love." Courtney pressed a hand against her chest. "But how in the world did we not know about her before you took this trip?"

"Because by the time I met you, Taylor was ancient history," I said as I sipped my own martini. "I wasn't still pining over her. In fact, I had barely thought about her in years until I bumped into her this spring."

"And how do you feel about her now?" Emily asked as she reached for her phone. She'd been checking it every few minutes to make sure she hadn't missed a call or text from the babysitter.

"A lot of things," I told her, going for another hearty sip of my martini. I didn't have to drive tonight, and maybe I needed to get drunk with my besties. Maybe it would help me figure out what to do with my life.

"Well, walk us through some of them," Courtney said.

"I think I love her," I said, surprising myself. But after just a few hours away, I already missed her with a fierceness I'd never felt after Sabrina left me. My life felt brighter and happier with Taylor in it and somehow empty without her.

"I think you do too," Emily said with an amused smile. "It's written all over your face every time to talk about her."

"Then how am I going to fix this? Even if I decline the offer from Bellair—which I'd really hate to do because it's a perfect fit for me and I'm kind of desperate for a steady paycheck—how do I not feel like I'm just giving up my life here for Taylor?"

"Is that how you feel?" Courtney asked.

"Part of me does," I admitted. "I think I could be happy in Vermont, but I don't know...this all happened so fast, and I feel like she's not willing to give me any time to figure how to make it work."

"I think you're both panicking right now," Emily said. "She's afraid of losing you if you stay here in Boston, and you're torn between your life here and what you had with her in Vermont. You both need to take a breath and be patient with each other."

"It felt an awful lot like she was about to break up with me on the phone," I said.

"Well, hopefully you'll be able to have a more civilized conversation face-to-face tomorrow," Emily said. "And if she's not willing to do that for you, then maybe this isn't meant to be."

I picked up my martini and downed the rest of the glass in a single gulp. Emily was right about one thing. I was definitely starting to panic. By the time I got back to my condo that night, I wasn't sure what to think, but one thing seemed certain. I had to tell Taylor how I felt about her when I got back to Vermont tomorrow. And maybe I needed to give myself some official closure with Sabrina while I was here.

To that end, I sent her a quick text to ask if she could meet me for coffee in the morning, and then I got in bed, exhausted but wired. I'd missed this luxurious mattress, but my bed felt cold and empty without Taylor and Violet in it. Sabrina responded,